Praise for Andrea Camilleri and the Montalbano Series

"In Sicily, where people do things as they please, Inspector Salvo Montalbano is a bona fide folk hero."
—*The New York Times Book Review*

"Hailing from the land of Umberto Eco and La Cosa Nostra, Montalbano can discuss a pointy-headed book like *Western Attitudes Toward Death* as unflinchingly as he can pore over crime-scene snuff photos. He throws together an extemporane-ous lunch of shrimp with lemon and oil as gracefully as he dodges advances from attractive women." —*Los Angeles Times*

"Camilleri can do a character's whole backstory in half a para-graph." —*The New Yorker*

"Camilleri is as crafty and charming a writer as his protagonist is an investigator." —*The Washington Post Book World*

"Like Mike Hammer or Sam Spade, Montalbano is the kind of guy who can't stay out of trouble. . . . Still, deftly and lovingly translated by Stephen Sartarelli, Camilleri makes it abundantly clear that under the gruff, sardonic exterior our inspector has a heart of gold, and that any outburst, fumbles, or threats are made only in the name of pursuing truth." —*The Nation*

"Sublime and darkly humorous . . . Camilleri balances his hero's personal and professional challenges perfectly and leaves the reader eager for more." —*Publishers Weekly* (starred review)

To access Penguin Readers Guides online, visit our Web site at www.penguinrandomhouse.com.

Also by Andrea Camilleri

Hunting Season
The Brewer of Preston
Montalbano's First Case and Other Stories

THE INSPECTOR MONTALBANO SERIES

The Shape of Water
The Terra-Cotta Dog
The Snack Thief
Voice of the Violin
Excursion to Tindari
The Smell of the Night
Rounding the Mark
The Patience of the Spider
The Paper Moon
August Heat
The Wings of the Sphinx
The Track of Sand
The Potter's Field
The Age of Doubt
The Dance of the Seagull
Treasure Hunt
Angelica's Smile
Game of Mirrors
A Beam of Light
A Voice in the Night
A Nest of Vipers
The Pyramid of Mud

© Elvira Giorgianni

DEATH AT SEA: MONTALBANO'S EARLY CASES

Andrea Camilleri, a bestseller in Italy and Germany, is the author of the popular Inspector Montalbano mystery series as well as historical novels set in nineteenth-century Sicily. His books have been made into Italian TV shows and translated into thirty-two languages. His thirteenth Montalbano novel, *The Potter's Field*, won the Crime Writers' Association International Dagger Award and was longlisted for the IMPAC Dublin Literary Award.

Stephen Sartarelli is an award-winning translator and the author of three books of poetry.

DEATH AT SEA:
MONTALBANO'S EARLY CASES

ANDREA CAMILLERI

Translated by Stephen Sartarelli

PENGUIN BOOKS

PENGUIN BOOKS

An imprint of Penguin Random House LLC
375 Hudson Street
New York, New York 10014
penguinrandomhouse.com

Originally published in Italian as *Morte in mare aperto e altre indagini
del giovane Montalbano* by Sellerio Editore, Palermo

LIBRARY OF CONGRESS CATALOGING-IN-PUBLICATION DATA
Names: Camilleri, Andrea. | Sartarelli, Stephen, 1954- translator.
Title: Death at sea : Montalbano's early cases / Andrea Camilleri ;
translated by Stephen Sartarelli.
Description: New York : Penguin Books, 2018.
Identifiers: LCCN 2018003930 (print) | LCCN 2018005879 (ebook) |
ISBN 9781101992111 (ebook) | ISBN 9780143108818
Subjects: LCSH: Montalbano, Salvo (Fictitious character)—Fiction. |
Police—Italy—Sicily—Fiction. | GSAFD: Mystery fiction
Classification: LCC PQ4863.A3894 (ebook) | LCC PQ4863.A3894 A2
2018 (print) | DDC 853/.914—dc23
LC record available at https://lccn.loc.gov/2018003930

Printed in the United States of America
1   3   5   7   9   10   8   6   4   2

Set in Bembo Std
Designed by Alice Sorensen

Contents

DEATH AT SEA:

MONTALBANO'S EARLY CASES

ROOM NUMBER 2

1

They were talking about this and that, sitting out on the veranda, when out of the blue, Livia made a statement that took Montalbano by surprise.

"When you get old you'll be so fixed in your habits, you'll be worse than an old cat," she said.

"Why do you say that?" the inspector asked, taken aback. And a little irritated. He didn't like to think about getting old.

"You may not realize it, but you're extremely methodical and orderly. If something is not in its proper place, you get upset. It puts you in a bad mood."

"Oh, come on!"

"You can't see it, but that's how you are. At Calogero's you always sit at the same table. And when you don't eat at Calogero's you always pick some restaurant to the west."

"To the west of what?"

"To the west of Vigàta. Don't pretend you don't know what I mean. Montereale, Fiacca . . . It's never, say, Montelusa or Fela . . . And yet there must be some nice places out that way. For example, I've been told that at San Vito, the Montelusa beach, there are at least two little restaurants that—"

"Did they give you their names?"

"Yes, the Anchor and the Skillet."

"Which one would you prefer?"

"Well, on the spur of the moment, I guess it would be the Skillet."

"I'll take you there this evening."

———

To Montalbano's immense satisfaction, the food was pig swill. On second thought, pigs must surely eat better than that. The establishment prided itself on its fried fish platter. But the inspector had a strong suspicion that the oil they used was motor oil, while the fish, which should have been crispy, was squishy and watery, as if they had cooked it the day before. And when Livia apologized for her mistake, Montalbano started laughing.

Once they'd finished eating, they both felt a pressing need to cleanse their palates, and so they went to a bar right on the beach to have a drink—a whisky for him, gin and tonic for her.

And just to show Livia that he wasn't as much a creature of habit as she said, on the drive back to Vigàta he took a different road from the usual one. They approached the first buildings in town from the elevated part, from where you could see the harbor and the calm sea below, reflecting a crescent moon.

"Look how beautiful! Let's stop for a minute," said Livia.

They got out of the car, and the inspector fired up a cigarette.

It was just past midnight, and the brightly lit mail boat for Lampedusa was putting about, ready to leave the harbor. A few fishing lamps flickered on the horizon.

Right behind them, a little detached from the other residences, was an old three-story building in rather dilapidated shape, with a bright neon sign on its crumbling façade that said: HOTEL PANORAMA. The front door was closed. Any late-arriving customers would have to ring the doorbell to get in.

Livia, enchanted by the clear, calm night, wanted to stay there and wait for the mail boat to reach the open sea before they left.

"I smell something burning," she said as they were walking back to the car.

"Me, too," said the inspector.

At that exact moment the front door of the hotel opened and somebody started shouting from inside:

"Fire! Fire! Everybody out! Quick! Everybody out!"

"You stay here," Montalbano ordered Livia, running towards the hotel.

Somewhere he thought he heard the sound of a car starting and then driving off at high speed. But he wasn't entirely sure, because there were also some strange crashing noises inside the hotel.

Upon entering the small, narrow entranceway, he saw, through the dense smoke, a great many tall and determined flames at the back of a short corridor. At the foot of the staircase in the middle of the hall, which led upstairs, stood a man in sleeveless T-shirt and underpants, still shouting:

"Come downstairs, all of you! Quick! Everybody outside!"

And, coming down the stairs at that moment—some in their underwear, others in pajamas, but all with shoes and clothes in hand and cursing—were three men, followed by another two, then yet another man. The latter was fully dressed and carrying a small suitcase. Apparently there were no women staying at that hotel.

The man at the foot of the stairs, who looked rather old, then turned to leave as well, when he spotted the inspector.

"Go out!"

"Who are you?"

"The owner."

"Are all your customers out of danger now?"

"Yes. They'd all come in for the night."

"Have you called the fire department?"

"Yes."

Suddenly the lights went out.

Outside there was already a noisy crowd of about twenty, who'd come out, in various states of undress, from the nearby residences.

"Take me away from here," said Livia, upset.

"They're all out of danger," said the inspector, to reassure her.

"I'm glad, but fires really scare me."

"Let's wait till we hear the firemen's siren," said Montalbano.

The following morning he decided to take the long way to work, the road that passed through the elevated part of town. He was suddenly dying of curiosity to find out how things had gone at the old hotel. Since the firemen had been late in arriving and taken a very long time to put out the flames, the building was now gutted. The inside had all burned up, leaving only the outer walls still standing, with holes that were once windows. Inside there were still a few firemen at work. The entire ruin was cordoned off. Four municipal cops were keeping the rubberneckers away. Montalbano gave them a dirty look. He hated the "disaster tourism" of those who rushed to witness the scene of a catastrophe or crime. And if someone had died during the fire, there would surely have been three times as many people trying to catch a glimpse of things.

A smell of burning still hung in the air. Overcome by a feeling of desolation, he left.

As he was parking the car in the station lot, he saw Augello race out of the building.

"Where are you off to?"

"I got a call from the fire chief, who told me they put out a fire last night . . ."

"I know all about it."

"He says it was a clear case of arson."

"Let me know when you get back."

He told Fazio how he'd happened to be with Livia outside the hotel the night before at the moment the fire broke out, and had seen its six customers fleeing.

"Do you know the owner?" he asked.

"Of course. His name is Aurelio Ciulla; he's a friend of my dad's."

"And that's all?"

"Chief, that hotel earns Ciulla next to nothing. He only

gets by with the help of subsidies from the city and regional governments . . ."

"Why doesn't he shut it down?"

"He's almost seventy now and he's fond of the place. And if he shuts it down, how's he gonna eat?"

"The firemen say it was arson. Do you think it could have been Ciulla himself who set the fire?"

"Bah! As far as I know, he's an honest man, he's never had any trouble with the law, he's a widower, he's never had any women, and has no vices, but I guess it's possible that, in desperation . . ."

Mimì Augello got back about two hours later. He looked quite fed up.

"Total waste of time. In short, this fire chief, after looking at the thing from all angles, in the end wasn't so sure that it was arson . . ."

"And why not?"

"The fire started in a rather large storeroom at the back of the hallway on the ground floor. It was used for storing bedclothes . . . And the fire chief found glass fragments of a bottle that had gasoline in it."

"So, a Molotov cocktail?" asked Montalbano.

"That's what it looked like to the fire chief."

"Does this storeroom have a window?"

"Yes. And it was open. But Signor Ciulla, the owner, told him he always kept a bottle of gasoline in there, which he used as a stain remover."

"And so?"

"And so there's no explanation, since the fire certainly

wasn't started by a short circuit. But the fire chief still had his doubts."

Montalbano thought about this for a moment. Then he said:

"Things for which there's no explanation get on my nerves."

"Mine, too," said Augello.

"You know what I say? I say call up Ciulla and tell him to be here at four o'clock this afternoon."

Augello went out and came back five minutes later.

"He says he'll be here at six, 'cause he has to talk with the insurance agent about the fire."

"What number did you call him at?"

"The one he gave me. He said it was his home number."

"So why was he sleeping at the hotel last night?"

"How should I know? You can ask him when he comes."

Aurelio Ciulla, now modestly dressed, was the man Montalbano had spoken to the night before, as the hotel was catching fire.

"Please sit down, Signor Ciulla. You've already met Inspector Augello and Detective Fazio. And you and I also met last night."

"Really? When?"

"I was near your hotel when the fire broke out, and so I went inside, and we spoke."

"I'm sorry, I don't remember anything."

"That's understandable. But tell me something. How come you were spending the night at your hotel?"

Ciulla looked at him in confusion.

"But it's my hotel!"

"I know that, but since you gave Inspector Augello your home phone number in Vigàta, I was just wond—"

"Ah, okay, I get it. I do that often, I'm not sure why. Sometimes I just feel like spending the night at the hotel, maybe 'cause it's too hot, or just because. Then at other times I don't feel like it."

"I see. Is your hotel insured?"

"Of course. And I'm all up to date on my payments. But today the insurance people called me to tell me they received the fire station's report, which says they think it was a case of arson, so they have to make sure it wasn't first."

"And that's exactly the reason I called you in. So we can try to understand together what—"

"But there's very little to understand, Inspector. Since the hotel earns nothing—actually, it loses money—everyone thinks I set the fire myself to get the insurance money."

"Well, you must admit . . ."

"At any rate I told the insurance people it's not up to me to prove that I had nothing to do with it."

"You're right; it's up them, and to us. And if it all went well, how much insurance would you get?"

"A pittance. About twenty million lire."

"Well, it's not exactly a pittance."

"But I can prove that I had nothing to do with burning down the hotel."

"How?"

"Do you know Curatolo, the engineer?"

Montalbano looked over at Fazio.

"He's the biggest real estate developer in the province," said Fazio.

"Last week he phoned me personally, wanting me to sell him the hotel. He offered me thirty million. He's interested in the fact that the area's suitable for building. So why would I want to set fire to the hotel and risk going to prison? If you don't believe me, you can call up Curatolo himself and see whether or not I'm telling the truth."

2

His argument was airtight. And this cleared him of any suspicion that he might be the culprit.

Still, the story of the engineer deserved at least to be checked out. With the current lust there was for buildable areas, one could not rule out the possibility that someone had resorted to dangerous measures.

"So how did you respond to Curatolo's offer?"

"I didn't say yes, and I didn't say no."

"So you waffled?"

"No, sir. He didn't want an immediate answer. He gave me fifteen days to think about it . . ."

"And now you'll accept his offer?"

"What else can I do?"

"If there hadn't been a fire, what would you have told him?"

"I probably would have said no. But . . ."

"But?"

"If you're thinking it was Engineer Curatolo who did it, to force me to sell the lot, you're dead wrong. He's not that kind of man."

The inspector looked at Fazio, who nodded at him, as if to confirm what Ciulla had said. Discarding that hypothesis, he immediately thought of another. He decided to broach the question head-on, without beating around the bush.

"The area where your hotel stood is Sinagra turf. Do you pay the racket?"

Ciulla didn't seem the least bit shocked by so direct a question.

"No, sir, I don't."

Montalbano reacted harshly.

"Don't you lie to me!"

"Inspector, the Mafia knows who has money and who doesn't. But now and then they do ask me to do them a favor, and I oblige them."

"What does that mean?"

"They'll ask me if someone can stay at the hotel for a night or two, free of charge."

"But do you take down their names?"

"Always. The terms of our arrangement are clear, and they've always respected them. I've never hidden any fugitives or people like that."

At this point Montalbano remembered something he'd seen the night before.

"Why were all your customers on the upper floors? Aren't there any rooms on the ground floor?"

"I can explain that. The ground floor consisted of a kitchen and a dining room that we closed years ago, then a small sitting room for customers, the office, two bathrooms, room number one, room number two, and the small room that caught fire. The two guest rooms are big and each has its own sitting area. I stay in room number one, while number two is almost always vacant, because it costs more than the others. The customers were all staying on the second floor for the simple reason that it's easier that way for the housekeeper to clean the rooms."

"Is there a parking lot?"

"Yes, behind the building, and it's pretty big."

"Is there a guard?"

"No. And since it's not guarded and out in the open, sometimes the neighbors park there, too. I just look the other way and don't say anything."

"Is there a back entrance to the hotel?"

"Yessir. It gives onto the parking lot."

"Let me get this straight. So any passerby on the street could just walk across the parking lot and come right up to the window of the storeroom without anyone stopping him?"

"That's exactly right."

"Were the registers and guest cards destroyed?"

"Yessir."

"Were the people who were there last night regular customers?"

"Four of them were; two were not."

"Do you by any chance remember their names?"

"Of course. I have a list for reimbursements from the damages. Only one doesn't want to be reimbursed, because he didn't lose anything, but I still know his first and last names."

"Please do me a favor and get Detective Fazio a copy of this list before the day is out."

11

"I can dictate it to him right now. I have an excellent memory."

"Where were the customers finally lodged?"

"At the Hotel Eden."

"Now just bear with me a little longer. Tell me exactly what was in that storeroom."

"Sheets, pillowcases, towels, napkins, clothes . . . and toilet paper, rags, mops . . ."

"All flammable stuff?"

"Yes."

"Was the door usually locked?"

"Of course not."

"How many people used to take what they needed from the storeroom?"

"Just one person, the housekeeper Ciccina, who's my only steady employee. She's very reliable and has been working for me for ten years. When we need an extra hand, I summon another housekeeper, Filippa. But yesterday only Ciccina was around, and she always goes home in the evening."

"Does Ciccina smoke?"

"No, sir."

"And you don't think that a customer, or perhaps a stranger, could have gone into that room?"

"Through the door?"

"Yes."

"I would have noticed."

"One last question: Was there anyone among your clients last night you weren't supposed to charge?"

Ciulla immediately understood what he meant.

"Yes. One."

"Is his name on the list?"

"Of course."

"Please point it out to Fazio. Who was it that told you he should get special treatment?"

"I got a call from Elio Sanvito."

"Signor Ciulla, for me that's enough for now. Please go with Fazio into his office. Good-bye, and thank you for your cooperation."

"What's going through your head?" asked Augello.

"If the fire chief says there's something that doesn't add up, he must have a reason. After talking to Ciulla we can rule out Ciulla himself, Engineer Curatolo, and the Mafia from the list of possible suspects. You think that's nothing?"

"It's a start. But where do the customers come in?"

"Isn't it possible that whoever set fire to the hotel might have had something against one of them?"

"It's possible, but it seems a little crazy to me that someone would commit a massacre just to kill one person."

"It wouldn't be the first time that has happened."

Fazio came back a few minutes later.

"Did he dictate the list to you?"

"Yes. But it's not enough for me."

"Why not?"

"Because Ciulla remembers their first and last names, but they're all from out of town and he doesn't know where any of them live. And he can't remember their phone numbers, either. But all the details are on the list he drew up for the reimbursements. He's bringing it to me in fifteen minutes, and I'll have a copy made."

"Who's Elio Sanvito?"

"Somebody from the Sinagra family. A kind of business representative. He manages what we might call their legitimate businesses."

"And who was the guy he brought to Ciulla's attention?"

"His name is Ignazio Scuderi, but I don't know him."

The whole affair was going to take a while to untangle. Montalbano glanced at his watch.

"Listen, it's getting late for me. We'll talk more about this tomorrow morning."

That evening Livia said nothing when the inspector took her out to eat at a restaurant west of Vigàta, the one on the beach at Montereale whose specialty was the quantity, variety, and excellence of their antipasti.

Only towards the end of the meal did Montalbano mention the possibility that the fire at the hotel might be a case of arson. She then asked the most logical and natural question.

"Do you suspect the owner?"

The inspector gave her a summary of what he'd been able to gather from his talk with Ciulla.

"So you're imagining that someone set fire to the storeroom from outside, through the window?"

"It's a possibility."

"Something's coming back to me," Livia said then. "At the time I didn't give it much importance, but now that you say . . ."

"Did you see something strange?"

"Well, you'd just gone into the hotel, and I was watching

you from inside the car when a car came really fast down the street on one side of the hotel, drove straight towards me, then made a left turn."

"You mean, in the direction of Montelusa?"

"Yes."

"I also heard a car start up and then drive off really fast. It's possible the guy who started the fire was inside."

Livia looked uncertain.

"What is it?"

"I don't know why, but I'm not sure it was a man at the wheel. But it's just an impression."

"I can't see a woman starting a fire like that."

"I must be mistaken."

The following morning Fazio came into work a little late, but to make up for it he had some interesting news.

"Chief, I have to tell you immediately that of the six customers on Ciulla's list, two are still in Vigàta and the others have left. However, I got the addresses and phone numbers for all of them."

"All right, then, let's start with those two. Who are they?"

"One of them's Ignazio Scuderi and he's a mechanic in Palermo; the other is Filippo Nuara, and he's a grain merchant from Favara. Scuderi is the person Ciulla said was sent to the hotel by Elio Sanvito, the Sinagra guy."

"We're going to have to look into this Scu—"

"I've already gathered a lot of information, Chief. Scuderi is a specialist who works for a Palermo company dealing in refrigerator trucks. He came to inspect and overhaul the trucks the Sinagras use to transport fish. I don't think he was involved in setting the fire."

Montalbano looked disappointed.

"And what can you tell me about the grain merchant?"

"Here things are a little less clear. What's a grain trader doing in a town like Vigàta, where nobody's exported any grain for over thirty years?"

"Did you find an answer to that question?"

"I rang up Ciulla and he told me this Nuara is a sort of regular customer who comes at the same time every month and stays for three days. When I asked him whether he gets any phone calls or meets with people, Ciulla said no. Since Nuara hadn't yet come out of his hotel, I told Gallo to stay close to him and report to me where he goes and who he meets with."

"And the four who've left, what can we do about them?"

"Chief, one of these four is a commercial traveler from Palermo; the second is a land surveyor who lives in Caltanissetta; the third is a real estate agent from Trapani; and the fourth a lawyer from Montelusa. All we can do is write to their local police stations for information."

"Are you kidding me? It'll take 'em three or four months just to answer, and that would already be asking a lot!"

"So what do you plan to do?"

"You've got the names, haven't you? And we've got friends all over Sicily, haven't we? Then let's turn to these friends privately. If we get any information worth taking seriously, we'll go in person to check it out. But let's not waste any time. In Palermo, I've got Inspector Lanuzza."

"In Caltanissetta, I've got Detective Truscia," Fazio countered.

Montalbano kept up his end.

"In Trapani there's Lo Verde. And Montelusa's no problem, there's an embarrassment of riches there."

There was a knock at the door. It was Gallo.

"Why'd you come back?" Fazio asked him.

"'Cause I did what I was supposed to do, and then I figured there was no point in continuing to tail the guy. I left Nuara as he was paying his hotel bill. He had a cab waiting for him and was about to leave."

"What did he do over the course of the morning?"

"He went out, called a cab, was driven to a florist's shop, bought a big bouquet of flowers, got back in the cab, went to the cemetery, put the bouquet down on a grave, said a prayer, and then went back to the hotel."

"Did you look at the name on the tombstone?"

"Yes. Giovanna Nuara née Rossotto."

"Call the church associated with it and ask the priest there whether they said a Mass yesterday for the soul of Signora Nuara."

Fazio called and confirmed. The poor husband, explained the priest, came every month to visit his dead wife.

3

The first to answer Montalbano's confidential request was Pippo Lo Verde of Trapani, who phoned at five p.m. the following day.

"Salvo, you wanted to know something about a real estate agent named Saverio Custonaci. Here's what I found out."

"Tell me."

"To tell you over the phone exactly what Custonaci does would be a little complicated. All I can say is that he's a person of interest, from your standpoint. Would you like to see with your own eyes what kind of man he is?"

"Very much."

"He's a methodical man and dines at the same restaurant every night. Where, among other things, one eats very well. All right if we meet at eight-thirty at the Bar Libertà?"

"Quite all right. Listen, would you mind if I brought my girlfriend along?"

"Not at all! On the contrary. That way I'll get to meet her."

Livia was very pleased to be invited. And she immediately hit it off with Lo Verde.

As they were walking to the restaurant, Lo Verde explained to Montalbano that Custonaci had been a skillful real estate agent in his youth, appreciated by everyone for his honesty and above all because during the negotiations over a sale, he knew how to remain neutral and impartial in his judgment.

So it was that one day, Sabato Sutera, a known mafioso who had an ongoing dispute with another mafioso, Ernesto Pilato, got the idea to ask Custonaci to serve as a kind of arbitrator to their quarrel. Custonaci accepted and brought his assignment to a conclusion that left both parties satisfied. Ever since that time, Custonaci had remained a mediator, but was no longer an agent. The interests for which he mediated no longer involved property but the sort of prickly disputes that arose between competing Mafia families and risked taking a bad turn.

And his fame grew so great that it spread beyond the confines of the province. By now he was summoned to every part of Sicily to work his magic.

"So he must certainly have gone to Vigàta to settle a dispute between the Sinagras and the Cuffaros," Lo Verde concluded.

And maybe the Cuffaros were not so satisfied with the results and mounted a nice little attack on him, thought Montalbano.

But he said nothing.

Apparently Lo Verde had set things up so that the table he'd reserved would be right next to that of Custonaci, who was already seated, waiting for his first course and looking around at the other clients, when the three of them came in.

He was a chubby man of about sixty, with an open, cordial face and an affable air that inspired confidence in the person in front of him. He dressed like a peasant, in fustian jacket and trousers, but had the manners of the well-bred. To the greeting of a man who'd just come in, he replied with a smile that looked somewhere between episcopal and paternal. He was perfectly calm and at ease.

It wasn't at all the attitude of someone who'd just been through an attack on his person.

"Is he alone?" Montalbano asked Lo Verde.

"Do you mean, does he have an escort?"

"Yes."

"No, he never does."

This confirmed the inspector's impression. Custonaci was not the target of the fire.

Meanwhile, the mediator had started eating.

Montalbano kept an eye on him, while eating in turn. And when he realized that Custonaci, having finished his fruit course, was getting ready to leave, he shot to his feet and, before the amazed eyes of Lo Verde and Livia, went over to the man's table.

"I'm sorry to trouble you."

Custonaci showed no sign of surprise.

"No trouble at all, Inspector Montalbano."

"Do you know me?"

"By sight, until a moment ago. Now I have the honor of knowing you in person. Please sit down."

Montalbano sat down.

"What can I do for you, Inspector? Ask me anything you like," said Custonaci, encouraging him with a smile.

"Thank you, you're very kind. You were in Vigàta the other night, when the hotel you were staying in—"

"Yes, that was quite unpleasant. And it might have gone worse for me, had room number two not been occupied. That's the one I usually ask for. It has a little sitting room that allows me to receive the people who come to meet me on so-called neutral ground."

Montalbano felt slightly bewildered.

Hadn't Ciulla told him that room number 2 was not occupied? He decided not to mention this to Custonaci.

"I see. But why do you imply you would have been in greater danger in room number two?"

"Because it's adjacent to the storeroom where the fire started. The smoke might have suffocated me in my sleep."

"Have you been told that the fire chief thinks it was arson?"

The inspector wasn't expecting the answer that Custonaci gave him, nor the almost indifferent tone in which he said it.

"That's not such a far-fetched surmise."

"So you agree?"

"Why, don't you, Inspector Montalbano? If you didn't, you wouldn't be wasting time talking to me."

"Am I wasting time talking to you?"

"That depends on what you want to know from me. If, to use an example, or just for the sake of argument, you want to know whether the fire was intended to kill me, you are just wasting your time."

"How can you be so sure?"

"From the simple fact that my mediation led to a resolution that met with the full satisfaction of both parties in question." He smiled. "They were both in full agreement; there were no objections of any sort. Have I made myself clear?"

"Quite clear."

Montalbano considered their discussion over, and was about to get up and go, when Custonaci stopped him with a hand gesture.

"May I ask a question myself?"

"Of course."

"You were in the hotel when we came downstairs on our way out. I saw you and recognized you in spite of the smoke and confusion. Do you remember how many customers we were in all?"

"Six."

"Precisely. That's how many I remember, too. And counting you and Ciulla, that makes eight of us."

He paused. Now he was no longer smiling.

"But then things don't add up."

"Why not?"

"Because if room number two was occupied, there should have been seven customers in all. These are numbers, Inspector. They're not opinions or theories. As far as I could tell, you seem to have arrived as soon as Ciulla started shouting. Did you see anyone come out of that room?"

"No."

"Nor did I. Which means there wasn't anyone staying in that room."

"And so?"

"And so why did Ciulla tell me it was occupied? You see, when I stay at that hotel, I pay duly and don't even ask for a discount. What reason could he have had to say I couldn't stay in room two? If I were you, I would try to find an explanation."

The following morning was crucial, because of three phone calls. One outgoing, and two incoming.

The first thing Montalbano did was to tell Fazio what Custonaci had said and to get Ciulla on the phone.

He didn't feel like wasting time with him and so got straight to the point.

"Last night I met Custonaci, the mediator, entirely by chance in Trapani, and we talked about the fire. Why did you tell him room number two was rented out when you told me the opposite?"

Ciulla replied at once.

"It's a delicate matter, Inspector."

"Delicate or not, answer my question first. Was room number two occupied or not?"

"Absolutely not, as I already told you. On the other hand, if it was rented out and nobody came out of the room, logically speaking the firemen should have found a corpse in there."

"Why did you tell Custonaci it was taken?"

"Inspector, Custonaci had come to my hotel three times in the last few months, and I always gave him room two, as he wanted. But the people he would receive there scared me just to look at them. So this time I asked myself: Why would I want people like that in my house? So I gave him an excuse. And as a result they had to meet wherever the hell they chose, but not at my place."

The explanation made sense, and Montalbano hung up.

"But how is it this man always finds a plausible excuse?"

He answered his own question.

"Either he's someone who never strays an inch from the straight and narrow path, or else he's a great big son of a bitch, even though he doesn't seem like one."

Fazio reported that he'd received news from Palermo first thing that morning about the traveling salesman, whose name was Pasquale Sanvito. The information said he was a man with a spotless reputation.

It said he was a serious, law-abiding citizen, a responsible provider for his family who earned his living honestly.

There was no reason in heaven or on earth to think anyone would want to start a fire to kill him.

Half an hour later, as they were still talking, Fazio's contact in Caltanissetta called him to tell him what he'd found on Guido Lopresti, the land surveyor.

"Look, Fazio, speaking from a professional point of view, this Lopresti is the kind of person you could say is irreproachable," said Detective Truscia. "And he's never out of work, because everyone thinks very highly of him."

"How about from the private point of view?"

"That's where things change radically."

"In what sense?"

"In the sense that he's a scoundrel. He's got a wife who's like a flower, young and beautiful, but that's not enough for him. He has another three women here, and another two or three in nearby towns. And since everybody knows this, sometimes things turn nasty between these women. And there you have it."

As Fazio hung up, he and Montalbano looked at each other in disappointment.

Clearly all these people were to be ruled out. There was only one of the hotel's customers left: the lawyer from Montelusa.

"Who should deal with this gentleman, you or me?" asked the inspector.

"I'll take care of it," said Fazio.

There was a knock at the door, and Mimì Augello came in.

4

"Good Lord, what happened to you two? You should see your faces! What happened? Did somebody die?"

"We've reached a dead end in the arson investigation," Fazio replied.

And since Mimì wanted to be filled in, the inspector told him the whole story.

"So there's only one of the six left?" Augello asked.

"Yes, a lawyer from Montelusa."

"A lawyer who lives in Montelusa?"

"Yes. What, have you gone deaf or something?"

"How odd!"

"Why? In your opinion there shouldn't be any lawyers living in Montelusa?"

"Come on, gimme a break!" said Mimì, offended. "It's you who said it. I'm trying to think seriously about this."

"Then let's hear your serious thoughts."

"My question is: Why, after taking care of business in Vigàta, didn't this lawyer just go on home to Montelusa after working hours? Even if he doesn't own a car and takes a cab home, he's still spending a lot less than a night at the hotel will cost him."

A solid argument, no two ways about it.

"Maybe he has a customer who works all day and can only see him late in the evening," ventured Fazio.

"No, that doesn't hold up," said Montalbano. "Mimì's right."

"What's this lawyer's name?" asked Augello.

"Ettore Manganaro," said Fazio.

"Aha!" exclaimed Mimì.

"What's 'aha' supposed to mean? Do you know him?"

"By name and by sight. He's one of the top criminal lawyers in Montelusa. He's about forty-five, rather elegant and well-mannered, and a bachelor. Which reinforces my suspicion and raises another question."

"And what's that?"

"Why would a man who earns as much as he does want to stay in a fourth-rate hotel? And on that note, I gotta go."

He got up and left.

"It's certainly true that a criminal lawyer like this Manganaro must have more than a few enemies," Fazio commented.

"By tomorrow evening I want you to tell me everything there is to know about this guy," the inspector ordered him. "So you should probably start right away."

Without a word, Fazio also left the room.

The information Fazio brought back was utterly generic in nature. Except for two details, one public, the other private. The former was that one of Manganaro's clients, Totuccio Gallinaro by name, a mafioso from the Sinagra clan who had been sentenced to thirty years, blamed Manganaro for the harsh penalty, accusing the lawyer of having made a deal with the prosecution. And Totuccio had publicly sworn he would make him pay for it.

The other detail was that the lawyer, after living for three years with the sister of a colleague of his, had thrown her out one month ago with no explanation, creating a kind of rift in the Order of Montelusan Lawyers.

"Did your friends tell you whether Totuccio's threat was anything to be taken seriously?"

"Oh, it's serious, all right."

"But do you really think the Sinagras would be ready to back Gallinaro up? I don't."

"Nah, I don't, either. But they can't do much to prevent some hothead friend of Gallinaro's from doing something stupid."

"Isn't it possible that Manganaro went to that hotel because he had an appointment with someone from the Sinagras? And he maybe even took advantage of the presence of the mediator, Custonaci, to get some kind of reassurance that Gallinaro's threat would be neutralized?"

"Sure, it's possible. But the question still remains: Why set fire to the hotel?"

At that exact moment an idea, still rather sketchy, began to stir in the inspector's brain.

"And what if we were wrong about everything?"

"What do you mean?" Fazio asked, taken aback.

"Wrong in the way we're conducting the investigation."

"Explain."

"Rather than investigate who was at the hotel, it might be better to find out who *wasn't* there."

Fazio gave him a confused look.

"Chief, except for those seven people—owner included—the rest of the world was outside. What are you saying?"

"That's not what I meant. I was conjecturing that maybe Ciulla sang us only half the Mass."

"I don't understand anything anymore."

"Try to follow my reasoning. Ciulla tells Custonaci that room number two is occupied. Right?"

"Right."

"Whereas he tells us it was free. Right?"

"Right."

"And what if he was telling the truth in both cases?"

"That's not possible! It was either free or it wasn't! There's no two ways about it!"

"But in fact there *are* two ways about it! Because at the moment Custonaci asks him about it, the room is reserved but the customer hasn't arrived yet; and when we ask him about it, the room is free because the customer has come and gone after a visit of only a few minutes."

"But you never saw that customer come out!"

"Do you know whether the back door, the one that gave onto the parking lot, was always locked or unlocked?"

"It was always locked. The customers had to ring the buzzer to enter."

"So it's possible that as soon as the fire broke out, this mystery customer went out the back door, which was also closer to where he was than the main door in front."

"Chief, your hypothesis doesn't hold water."

"Why not?"

"Because the back door, being right next to the store-room, was unusable."

"That doesn't matter. I want to continue down this path."

"How?"

"Call all six customers and have them tell you, in this order, what day and at what time of day they got to the hotel, at what hour they came in on the night of the fire, and anything, no matter how minor, they managed to see or hear in the minutes preceding the outbreak of the fire."

Two hours later, the inspector had their answers. The

conscientious Fazio had written them all down on a sheet of paper that he'd left on Montalbano's desk.

1. Ignazio Scuderi, mechanic.
Arrived two days before the fire, came back to the hotel at
10:30 p.m. on the night of the fire. Saw and heard noth-
ing unusual.

2. Filippo Nuara, grain merchant.
Arrived the day before, came back to his room at 10:00 p.m.
Saw and heard nothing.

3. Saverio Custonaci, mediator.
Arrived at 9:00 on the morning of the same day and went
out half an hour later. Returned at 11:00 p.m. and
went right to sleep. Saw and heard nothing.

4. Pasquale Sanvito, traveling salesman.
Arrived three days earlier, came back at about 10:00 p.m.
Heard and saw nothing.

5. Ettore Manganaro, lawyer.
Arrived the evening of the fire, at about 11:30 p.m.
Though awake and still dressed when the fire broke out, he
saw and heard nothing.

6. Guido Lopresti, surveyor.
Arrived the day before, got back to the hotel at about
*11:30 p.m.****

"What are the three asterisks supposed to mean?"

"They mean that Lopresti told me a whole lot of things that were too complicated to write down."

"Tell me now."

"Well, he said that when he got back to the hotel at

eleven-thirty he wanted to ask Ciulla for a wake-up call at six the following morning, but he had to wait a good five minutes because Ciulla was busy chatting with Manganaro, the lawyer, whom he recognized by sight and who must have arrived just before that because he still had his overnight bag in his hand. The lawyer then went upstairs to his room, and after talking with Ciulla, Lopresti himself went to bed."

"That doesn't seem like such a—"

"Wait. I haven't come to the best part yet. Lopresti's room was the one directly above the sitting area of room number two. He'd just gotten undressed—so it was about ten minutes to twelve—when he heard a car pull up in the lot outside, then about a minute later the doorbell to the back door rang. It was clearly a customer who'd just arrived. Not fifteen minutes later, he heard the window of the sitting area of room two being opened violently, and almost immediately afterwards, he heard Ciulla's voice shouting: 'Fire!'"

Montalbano slapped himself hard on the forehead.

"The window!"

"What do you mean?"

"I mean the customer who was so briefly in room number two left through the window! It's all clear to me now!"

"Then please make it clear to me, too."

"Later. First I want you to find out something of capital importance to me: What kind of relations does Ciulla have, or has Ciulla had, with Manganaro, the lawyer? I want to know within the hour. Now get out of here."

Fazio must have broken some kind of record. An hour and fifteen minutes later, he was back.

Twenty years earlier, Ciulla's younger brother, Agostino, was charged with taking part in an armed robbery in which someone had died. Agostino had always claimed his innocence, and Manganaro, still cutting his teeth at the time, defended him and won him a full acquittal, earning Ciulla's endless gratitude.

"Go get him and bring him here to me!"

"Who?"

"Ciulla."

Ciulla was as calm and collected as usual.

"Please listen to me," said the inspector, "and I'll tell you what I think happened. On the morning of the day of the fire, you get a phone call from Manganaro, the lawyer, who tells you he needs to meet with a fugitive in the safest place possible. You reserve room number two for the fugitive, and another room upstairs for the lawyer. Manganaro arrives with his car at eleven-thirty that evening, probably tells you that the fugitive will be arriving shortly, also by car, and will buzz at the back door. Which is exactly what happens. But the lawyer doesn't have time to meet the fugitive, because, in the meantime, the fire breaks out. You rush to room number two to let the fugitive escape through the window in the sitting room. The fire itself was probably started by someone who didn't want that meeting to take place. Have you followed me?"

"Yes, perfectly."

"Do you realize that I can throw you in jail on two very serious charges?"

"I realize that. But, if you'll allow me, I'd like to tell you a story I like a lot better than yours. A hotel manager gets a phone call from a lawyer whom he worships. A month earlier, this lawyer fell madly in love with a woman separated from her husband but whose ex-mate is still extremely jealous. That evening, the two finally have an opportunity to spend the night together in peace. And so the hotel manager leaves room number two available to them. The lawyer arrives, talks to the manager, and retires to his room. Five minutes later, the back-door buzzer rings. The manager opens the door and sees the woman there. The manager closes the door and shows her to her room. The lady is nervous and asks for a bottle of water and a glass. The manager goes and gets these for her. When he returns, the woman informs him that there's no running water in the bathroom sink. While the manager is doing his best to accommodate her, the woman comes into the bathroom and tells him there's a strong smell of smoke. The manager leaves the room and sees that the storeroom has caught fire and it's not the sort of thing a small extinguisher can handle. And so he has the woman escape out the window and starts shouting. What do you think?"

"I think you're right, your story's a lot better than mine. So, in your opinion, it was the lady's ex-husband who set fire to the place?"

"In the lawyer's opinion, too. And he went and talked to the husband. Who says he was desperate. He'd followed his wife and when he realized she was going to meet with the lawyer, he lost his head. He had a newspaper in his jacket pocket, and so he lit it and threw it in through the storeroom window. He's willing to pay for the damages. He's willing to do anything. It was just a moment of madness, he said. He's a good man. He didn't realize he could have caused a massacre. He just wanted to break up that meeting. The lawyer's not going to press charges, and I'm not, either. What are we going to do, Inspector?"

For the first time in his life, Montalbano didn't know how to respond.

DOUBLE INVESTIGATION

1

Ernesto Guarraci, forty-five years old, a surveyor by trade and official consultant to city hall for urban development and to the provincial government for large public land projects, was in reality a do-nothing with no desire whatsoever to do anything. Actually, no. There was one thing he never tired of doing: playing poker from morning till night, and vice versa, and almost always losing.

He was also a have-nothing. But he got by just fine, in that he'd been married for ten years to Giovanna Bonocore, a rich woman who made sure he always went around with a full wallet that sang in the morning and wept in the evening.

One day, a Wednesday, Signora Giovanna announced to her husband that she wanted to go and visit her sister Lia, who lived in Caltanissetta, on Saturday. Ernesto replied that he couldn't drive her there because on Saturday afternoon he needed the car to go to Fiacca.

Giovanna replied that she would take the train that left Vigàta at six in the morning and would be home by eight that evening. Ernesto would have to drive her to the station to catch the train and then pick her up on her return.

As he later declared to Montalbano, when filing a missing persons' report, Ernesto Guarraci had not dropped his wife off directly outside the station, since some ongoing construction work made that too complicated; rather, he'd left her at the entrance to the underpass in Via Lincoln. And then he'd gone home.

At around nine-thirty he'd received a phone call from his worried sister-in-law, Lia.

"I've been waiting at the station for Giovanna since seven this morning. Why isn't she here yet?"

"What do you mean? She never got there?! But she definitely left! I drove her to the station myself!"

"Ernè, I'm in no mood for joking. Let me talk to Giovanna."

"But I tell you she left!"

Wasting no time, Ernesto Guarraci dashed off to the train station. At the only open booth, behind the glass, was a fiftyish woman, Signora Sferlazza, who knew Giovanna well. She swore up and down to the surveyor that she had not seen his wife that morning, and that she certainly hadn't come in and bought a ticket.

Therefore Signora Giovanna must have disappeared in the underpass, which had two exits in addition to the one that came out at the station: one which led to Via Crocilla and the other to Via Vespucci.

This underpass was a public works project of utterly no use to the public, like so many that were undertaken during those years. In fact they were useful only to the politicians who'd wanted them in order to line their pockets, and to the contractors who built them so they could skim off the profit from the cheap materials they used.

And indeed, just a few months after completion, thanks to leaks and poor workmanship, the underpass had turned into a cross between a small lake and a latrine.

Hardly anyone ever used it.

Fazio reported to Montalbano that there was a persistent rumor around town that Signora Giovanna had disappeared of her own volition.

The signora, who was a fine-looking woman of about forty and quite appetizing, had supposedly been the mistress of a certain Dr. Curatolo, and the gossips said that the two had decided to run away and live together. But there was one fact that undermined this widespread opinion, which was that Dr. Curatolo had never left Vigàta, not even for a day.

So how can two people live together if one is here and the other is over there?

Weighing his options, Montalbano quietly summoned the doctor. He was a handsome, distinguished-looking man, but with nerves as taut as violin strings.

"Thank you, Doctor, for accepting my invitation to come and see me," said the inspector. "I understand how hard it must be for you to talk about such a delicate matter . . ."

"Actually, it is I who must thank you, Inspector. This way I can finally clear things up. Giovanna and I were lovers, but neither of us had any serious intention to abandon our respective families to go off and live in another town. If she hadn't disappeared, our relationship would have quietly continued."

"So you're telling me you had nothing to do with her disappearance?"

"That's correct. It took me by surprise, too. I tried to explain that to Ernesto—"

"You met?!"

"He came to my medical office on his own initiative.

And he made a big scene right in front of my patients. That was how everyone in Vigàta came to know of our affair."

"Can you tell me who it was that informed her husband?"

"He said he'd received an anonymous letter, but in fact he'd known about it for at least a year—Giovanna told me herself—and looked the other way. Anyway, he had a lover, too, Giovanna told me, a certain Giuliana."

"Please don't be offended by what I'm about to ask you."

"Don't worry about that."

"Isn't it possible that Giovanna, aside from you, had another man?"

"I would tend to rule that out."

"Why?"

Dr. Curatolo seemed embarrassed.

"In the last few months, our relationship underwent—how shall I put it?—a profound transformation."

"Meaning?"

The doctor cleared his throat before answering.

"For Giovanna, our affair became something serious. Let's just say she . . . she fell in love with me."

"And how about you?"

"No."

Sharp and dry, like a rifle shot.

"Sorry to insist, but how in love was she?"

"She'd started hinting at the possibility of leaving her husband."

"And how did you react?"

"I talked her out of it. And it didn't take much on my part because I could tell she wasn't terribly determined . . . More than anything else, I think it was a manifestation of an unattainable desire, actually."

"And what do you yourself make of her disappearance?"

"I would certainly rule out any kind of amnesia or lapse of memory."

"And so?"

"Didn't Guarraci tell you why Giovanna was going to see her sister that Saturday?"

"No. I had the sense she went there often."

"That's true. But that Saturday there was a precise reason, and Giovanna told it to me in confidence. Lia had asked her for a large sum of money for her husband, whose business was in trouble."

"Do you know how much?"

"About twenty million lire."

Montalbano balked. Not exactly peanuts.

"And Giovanna was inclined to comply . . ."

"She was more than inclined. They're twins and care the world for each other."

Montalbano got in his car and went to see Signora Lia. Her husband, Gaspare Guarnotta, was also there. Through her tears Lia confirmed what the doctor had said. And she pointed out that the exact amount was eighteen million lire. But it had to be in cash.

Montalbano didn't understand.

"I'm sorry, but wouldn't it have been better just to wire the money or write a few checks?"

Signora Lia looked at her husband and said nothing. Signor Guarnotta made a face that looked half-embarrassed and half-offended.

"You know how it is . . ."

"No, I don't know how it is."

"I'm forced to steer clear of the local banks. My accounts are in the red. The risk is that they might seize the money as a partial reimbursement of my debt."

"I see. So Signora Giovanna, when leaving the house, had eighteen million lire in the large handbag that disappeared with her?"

"No, no," said Signora Lia. "I think she only took out a million on Friday morning, which would have let Gaspare pay a bill whose deadline was Monday. Shortly thereafter, she was going to give us another three or four. On Saturday she was going to bring us more money and find out how much the next payments should be and how to get them to us. She was supposed to meet with Gaspare so that my brother-in-law wouldn't find out."

"So Guarraci was in the dark as to—"

"Yes . . . My sister had no reason to tell him what she did with her money. They sometimes quarreled over this."

"She didn't trust her husband?"

"I don't think it was a lack of trust. Giovanna's always been that way, even as a little girl. Her things were hers, and nobody else had any say in the matter."

Guarraci, the surveyor, was taken aback.

"Eighteen million, to her sister Lia? She'd never said anything to me about that! Because, if she had . . ."

"You would have prevented her?"

"I would have tried! That's throwing money away! Guarnotta's a born loser!"

"But where did your wife keep her checkbooks, balance sheets, and cash?"

"In a small wall safe hidden behind a picture hanging in the entrance hall."

"Do you have the key or the combination?"

"Never have."

"Do you know whether they're somewhere in the house?"

"They're not. My wife used to carry the key around her neck, on a little chain."

The inspector went to have a look at the safe. It had a double lock, one that opened with a key, and the other with a combination. Later, with the prosecutor's permission, he had the safe opened by a technician from Forensics.

Between checking and savings accounts and Treasury bonds, Signora Giovanna had about sixty million lire. The judge impounded it all.

Fazio, who'd been keeping busy, had found a witness, the street sweeper, Totò Faticato, who said that he'd seen Guarraci's car stop outside the underpass at fifteen minutes to six that morning. Signora Giovanna had stepped out of the car, a large purse slung across her shoulders, and started going down the stairs, and the car had immediately started to turn around. He even remembered that, while making this maneuver, the surveyor had practically run over Tano Alletto, who had just got off work from his job as a night guard.

Six days later, Alletto was still in a rage about it.

"He nearly killed me, the fucking idiot! He got out of the car, apologized, told me he was Guarraci, the surveyor, and that he'd nodded off for second."

The street sweeper, who'd kept on working in the area

41

for another fifteen minutes, swore that he hadn't seen anyone come out of the exit of the underpass onto Via Vespucci. He couldn't say anything about the other exit, which came out on Via Crocilla, because he couldn't see it from where he was. Via Crocilla was a short street with ten houses on either side. And two factories at the end. It was on the distant outskirts of town, where the countryside began. Montalbano and Fazio questioned practically everyone who lived in those twenty houses. Nobody had seen anything.

Only Signora Annunziata Locascio, who lived on the ground floor of the building closest to the underpass, had heard anything.

"Since I always get up around five-thirty every morning, about ten minutes after I got out of bed I heard a car drive up really fast and then screech to a halt. So I looked out the window and saw two men get out of the car and go down into the underpass."

"Did you notice whether there was a third man still at the wheel?"

"No, sir, there were just those two."

"Do you remember what kind of car it was? And did you get a look at the license plate?"

"I don't know the first thing about cars, and I didn't see the license plate. It was a big car, bottle green and all banged up. One of the rear fenders was half-missing."

"Then what?"

"Then I heard it drive off again, even faster than when it arrived; it must have been about five or ten minutes to six, but in any case it was definitely before six, 'cause that's when I wake up my husband and bring him coffee."

This, more or less, was where the investigation had stood when it ground to a halt.

2

On the other hand, an investigation into a band of thieves specializing in burgling the shops of watchmakers and jewelers had gone well and come to a satisfying conclusion.

Montalbano had assigned the case to Mimì Augello, who might well be an indolent skirt chaser, but when he put his all into an investigation, he showed what an excellent cop he really was. After three months' work he'd managed to arrest all eight members of the gang and recover most of the stolen goods.

The same day the case was closed, a Thursday, Commissioner Burlando phoned the inspector.

"Could you bring your second-in-command, Augello, to my office tomorrow evening around seven-thirty? I'd like to congratulate him."

At seven the following evening Montalbano headed off to Montelusa with Augello at his side. Those had been torrid days, and the heat still hadn't let up. Most people had already left for the weekend, and the roads were nearly deserted.

At a certain point, as they were chatting, a motorcycle with two men on it passed them at a moderate speed. As soon as it overtook them, the motorbike slowed down, made a U-turn, and came back towards them.

"Look at those assholes!" Montalbano said.

Moments later the motorcycle came up beside them again, passed them, and slowed down again.

The man sitting in back turned around.

"Salvo, watch out!" Augello shouted.

And at that same moment the man fired a gun. Four shots. As the windshield exploded, Montalbano skidded, running off the road, with half the car ending up in a ditch.

He felt a strong pain in his chest, but saw no wound. The motorcycle had meanwhile driven away. When he looked at Mimì he got scared. His face was covered in blood, and he was either dead or had fainted. Then he saw that the blood was coming from a cut in his forehead and felt reassured.

The first to deliver first aid was a municipal cop from Vigàta who happened to drive past.

Ten minutes later two ambulances arrived. Augello in the meantime had recovered. They were taken to Montelusa Hospital and put in the same room.

The doctors said that Montalbano had cracked two ribs crashing against the steering wheel, while Augello had a wide but not deep wound caused by a shard of glass from the windshield. It really couldn't have gone any better for them . . .

The first to arrive was the commissioner. He was upset and emotional, embracing both Montalbano and Augello and saying that he was assigning the investigation of the attack to Inspector Cusimato, chief of the Flying Squad.

Then Pasquano arrived.

"I so would have loved to perform your autopsy!" he said to Montalbano.

Then the entire Vigàta police department arrived, with Fazio leading the way.

Meanwhile the TV news programs reported the attack.

The following morning, the doctors examined the patients and told them they could go home. Gallo came to pick them up in a squad car. Augello had his head wrapped in bandages that looked like a grand vizier's turban. Montalbano was taken home to Marinella. He found Adelina there, in tears.

"My Gah, I's so a-scared!"

She brought an armchair out onto the veranda, had him sit down, set the table, and then served him.

Around four, Livia arrived. Adelina, who couldn't stand the sight of her, said good-bye and left. Around half past five, Fazio arrived, and at six Cusimato phoned, asking if he could drop by. Half an hour later he was knocking at the door. Montalbano told Fazio to stay.

Cusimato was an intelligent man, so intelligent, in fact, that instead of asking any questions, he said to Montalbano:

"You go ahead and talk."

"The journalists are all convinced it was a Mafia hit."

"You don't agree."

"No. For a very simple reason. If it had been the Mafia, I wouldn't be here talking to you. At this point, you would all be making funeral arrangements."

"But the fact remains that they followed you from the moment you came out of headquarters . . ."

"No! Nobody followed me. It wasn't even a premeditated act."

"How can you say that?"

"The two guys on the motorbike were not following us. They were going their own way. When they passed my car, they recognized me. Wanting to be sure it was me, they made a U-turn and only then did they pass me again in order to shoot me. We'd crossed paths by accident, I'm convinced of it. But tell me something, did you have a look at my car?"

"Of course."

"Where did the shots end up?"

"One punctured the left fender, another went through the radiator, and the third hit the windshield right in the middle."

"And the fourth?"

"There was a fourth shot?"

"Yes, and it didn't even hit the car. You can't really say the guy was a good shot."

"Did you manage to see his face?"

"He was wearing a helmet. And what have you got to tell me?"

"What should I have? I'm going to talk to Augello now. Maybe he'll remember the license number."

"Mimì? You've gotta be kidding!"

"Listen, what do you say if I set up a guard service for you for the time you'll be here without—"

"Not in a million years!" the inspector said, interrupting him.

As soon as Cusimato left, Fazio came in.

"Tell me what you want me to do, Chief," he said.

"I haven't got the slightest idea," Montalbano replied.

"When do you think you'll come back to the office?"

"The doctors told me to move as little as possible for at least a week, but I may just lose my mind. So I'll stay put until tomorrow. Then I'll give you a ring and you can send a car to get me."

He couldn't make love to Livia that evening, either, even though he really wanted to.

At ten o'clock the following morning he received a phone call from Guttadauro, the lawyer and notorious consigliere for one of the two Mafia families of Vigàta.

The lawyer spoke in the plural, meaning that he was speaking on behalf of a third party.

"Inspector Montalbano, you cannot imagine the joy we felt upon learning that that cowardly attack on you didn't . . ."

About an hour later, Piscopo, the lawyer and consigliere for the other family, also called. And he, too, used the plural.

"Inspector, we rejoiced when we heard that you came out of it relatively unharmed, and so we wanted to express our . . ."

This was confirmation of what he'd been thinking. The Mafia was keen to let him know that they had nothing to do with the attempted murder.

He spent the rest of the day in the armchair. Livia, having ordered lunch from Calogero's trattoria, took a taxi to pick it up. That meal did more for Montalbano than any treatment could have done.

The following morning he sent for a car, and Gallo showed up and drove him to the station.

Catarella, in tears, ran up to the car to open the door for him, helped him out, and accompanied him all the way to his office, treating him as if he was severely disabled. Then Fazio appeared.

"Where's Augello?"

"He had such a bad headache, the doctor told him to take a week off."

As if he wouldn't take advantage of the situation!

"Listen, Fazio. Yesterday, having nothing better to do, I thought a long time about Signora Guarraci's disappearance. My question is this: How many people knew that she would be taking the six a.m. train on Saturday?"

"I was wondering the same thing, Chief. And I asked around a little. Two people definitely knew. Her husband and the cleaning lady, whose name is Trisina Brucato."

"So you've spoken with this Trisina?"

"Of course. And she told me she knew the signora had a million lire in cash in her purse."

"You don't think . . ."

"She seemed like an honest woman to me."

Unlikely that Fazio would have a mistaken impression.

"So that leaves only the husband. Do you know anything about his supposed girlfriend?"

"Her name is Giuliana Loschiavo. She's twenty years old and a marvel to look at. Apparently she's got Guarraci going out of his mind."

"Why?"

"Because this Giuliana's got a thing for another guy."

"Do you know who?"

"Yes, I do: Stefano Di Giovanni, the biggest fishmonger in town. Also married. The girl divides her time equally between the two, but Guarraci wants exclusive rights."

"And she's probably ready to go with the best offer. Could you have her here for four o'clock this afternoon?"

———

Livia arrived in a car she'd rented and took him to Calogero's.

When they finished, she drove him back to the station.

Giuliana Loschiavo showed up at four o'clock sharp. Fazio showed her into the inspector's office and sat down after the girl took her place in front of the desk.

She was a fine specimen of femininity and didn't seem the least bit intimidated to find herself in front of a police inspector. Indeed she was the first to speak.

"I know why you wanted to see me."

"Let's see if you've guessed right."

"Since Guarraci's wife has disappeared, you wanted to know about my affair with him. Is that right?"

"That's right."

"Well, look, Inspector. We haven't seen each other for two months. It was I who left him."

"Why?"

"Because he'd promised me he and his wife would separate, and we would go somewhere and live together, but in the end he never kept his word."

Montalbano couldn't resist letting slip a little jab.

"So then you must also have left Signor Di Giovanni."

The girl gave a hearty laugh.

"No, I haven't left Stefano."

"Has he separated from his wife?"

"No, but he never promised me he would."

Made perfect sense.

"Since his wife's disappearance, has Guarraci tried to get in touch with you?"

"Not yet. But I'm sure he will, sooner or later."

When Fazio returned after showing the girl out, he found Montalbano lost in thought.

"So, what do you think?" he asked him.

"You heard her yourself, didn't you? Without realizing it, this Giuliana let us know that Guarraci had a good motive for wanting to get rid of his wife. But what the girl doesn't know is that Guarraci doesn't have a cent to his name, and that if he leaves his wife he'll be left high and dry. Therefore he's most likely the one who set up the disappearance. That way he still keeps his right to the inheritance."

"You may be right."

"Here's a question. What reason did he have for giving his first and last name to the night guard he almost ran over with his car? The answer is: The only possible reason is that he wanted to have a witness who could swear that he was on his way home after dropping his wife off outside the underpass and therefore had nothing to do with the disappearance."

"So he had accomplices working for him."

"Which would be the two guys who arrived in the big car on Via Crocilla. Listen: As of this moment, we have to keep an eye on Guarraci day and night."

3

That evening, after being dropped off at home, he found Livia on the veranda with a book in her hand.

"What are you reading?"

"A novel by Sciascia, *To Each His Own*. It was published many years ago. I'm on the last pages."

He hadn't read it, either.

"I'd like to read it when you're done."

Cusimato rang just as they were about to go out to eat.

"The very latest developments. The motorbike from which the assassins shot at you ran over a peasant about four kilometers down the road, afterwards, but without doing much harm. The peasant gave a carabiniere what he thought was the license number. I found this out from a captain of the force who's a friend of mine. The only problem is there's no license plate with that number."

"Those don't seem like such great results to me."

"Wait. Then I took the number myself and hired an expert to do a little combinatorial analysis; he'll check each new combination to see whether the number corresponds to any existing license plate."

The inspector didn't understand a word of this.

"At any rate, it'll take a little time," Cusimato continued.

"Best of luck," said Montalbano.

———

"I want to talk to you," Fazio said the following day, appearing in the inspector's office as soon as Montalbano had gone in.

"So talk to me."

"There's something that didn't make sense to me, and I confirmed it last night. It's already been about twenty days since Signora Giovanna disappeared, but how is it that Guarraci keeps on gambling and keeps on losing big-time?"

"Explain."

"Chief, it's known all over town that Signora Giovanna used to refill her husband's wallet every Monday morning. With as much cash as he needed for the week. But now a good three weeks have gone by! So my question is: Who's giving him this money? Where's he getting it?"

"Well done, Fazio!" Montalbano exclaimed as another idea surfaced in his brain. "What's the name of the bank where Signora Giovanna keeps her money?" he asked.

"Banca Popolare di Montelusa."

He knew the manager. It was worth a try. And even if all he got was a polite refusal, one way or another, he would still manage to find out what he wanted to know.

"I'm going out. I'll be back soon."

The bank manager seemed reluctant at first. But the inspector didn't feel like wasting time.

"Have you received the memo from the prosecutor's office that all of Signora Guarraci's assets have been frozen?"

"Yes, and I don't understand the reason for—"

"It's quite simple. The courts decided to freeze her assets in case her disappearance turns out to be a kidnapping for ransom. They've chosen to take a hard line."

"I understand."

"For this reason your bank will be required to send its balance statement for this month to the prosecutor's office, something they'll ask you to do within the next few days. And I'll be having a look at it, too. All I'm asking you now is to let me have an advance look at it, which would save me precious time."

The manager had been persuaded.

It turned out that on her last visit, Signora Giovanna had withdrawn no less than five million lire.

"Was that normal for her?"

"Well, no. Signora Guarraci normally withdrew three or

four hundred thousand lire every two weeks, though sometimes the sum was more substantial. But never as much as that last time."

"She took out five million to spare herself the trouble of going back to the bank within a few days. She left four million in her safe, assured that her husband didn't know where she'd hidden the second key, the extra one. Whereas in fact Guarraci knew perfectly well where she kept it, and knowing that his wife would never return, he opened the safe and grabbed the money. And, in fact, we didn't find a single lira in cash in there."

"He would have needed at least part of the money to pay off his accomplices."

"I don't think so. I think he probably paid his accomplices by telling them to take the million they would find in her purse."

"If only we could prove he has this key in his possession . . ."

"Well, he certainly doesn't have it anymore. He's thrown it away by now. What would be the point of hanging on to evidence against him when there's nothing left in the safe?"

"You're right. And so?"

"Just be patient. If things are the way I think they are, part two of the show is about to begin."

"Meaning?"

"Meaning that Guarraci can't waste too much time. He's short on cash and needs to get his hands on that inheritance as soon as possible. Part two, which will begin very soon, will consist of the discovery of Signora Giovanna's body. She will be found to have been killed during a robbery. And that's where I'm hoping Guarraci makes a false move."

———

At eight o'clock that evening, while waiting for Livia to finish getting dressed, he turned on the television. On the TeleVigàta channel, Pippo Ragonese was interviewing Guarraci.

". . . I can only lament the extreme slowness of the investigation. The continued freeze on my wife's assets is making life extremely difficult for me."

"It's possible that Inspector Montalbano, following the attempt on his life, is thinking more about his own personal matters than about those of us citizens."

"If that's the case, then the commissioner would do well to turn the case over to someone else. How can it be that twenty days later I still know nothing and nobody will deign to keep me abreast of developments? That's no way to do things . . ."

"I'm ready," said Livia.

Montalbano turned off the set, and they went out to eat. When they returned—rather late because they'd gone to a restaurant in Fiacca—the inspector started reading the Sciascia novel. He even brought it with him to bed, but had to stop reading when Livia protested that the light was keeping her awake.

At seven o'clock the following morning, the phone rang.

Livia mumbled and Montalbano, cursing the saints, went and answered.

"It's Fazio, Chief. A body's been found. I'm on my way there, and meanwhile I'm sending Gallo to pick you up."

The inspector washed, got dressed, drank a pint of espresso, and went and kissed Livia. Gallo arrived, and they drove off.

"Where are we going?"

"Out to the country, Chief."

When they got to Vigàta, Gallo took Via Lincoln, passed by the train station, turned onto Via Crocilla, took it to the end, took one of the three unpaved roads that led down from the elevated part of Vigàta to the countryside below, and after they'd gone about a kilometer, Montalbano saw Fazio's car alongside a squad car. Near them was a small van with a refrigerator on its roof.

The area was completely deserted, partly because it was a huge dumping site.

Gallo pulled up, the inspector got out, and Fazio came towards them.

"It's Signora Guarraci, isn't it?"

"How'd you guess?"

"And how'd you manage to identify her?"

"They were kind enough to leave her purse near the corpse with her ID inside."

"Have you called the circus?"

"Yup."

"Who found the body?"

"Lemme get him for you."

He cupped his hands around his mouth.

"Signor Danzuso!"

The door of the van opened and a very thin young man of about thirty came out, almost six and a half feet tall. He immediately protested.

"I have to go to work! I can't waste the whole morning here!"

"Did you get his name and address?" the inspector asked Fazio, who nodded in the affirmative.

"What were you doing here?" he asked the young man.

"We came here in two cars, me and my friend Parrinello, me to throw away my refrigerator, him to get rid of a washing machine. I gave him a hand with the washer, but as we were getting rid of it, we saw the dead body. So Parrinello got in his car and went to call you guys, while I, like the stupid shit I am, stayed behind to wait for you, without being able to get rid of my fridge. And what am I gonna do with it now?"

"You're going to take it back home with you."

Danzuso looked at him in shock, and then, without a word, turned his back, ran towards his van, got inside, started it up, and drove off.

"Let's go and have a look," said the inspector.

The corpse lay stretched out, in an orderly state, with her purse beside it.

"They didn't bother to hide her. Actually, they made sure to put her where she would be seen," the inspector observed.

There was a livid bruise around the dead woman's neck.

"They strangled her, kept the corpse hidden away, then brought it here last night. Otherwise the dogs and rats would have made mincemeat of it. And in fact, aside from a few signs of decomposition, there's no visible damage to the body."

At that moment Dr. Pasquano arrived. In a dark mood, he grumbled a greeting and crouched down beside the dead woman. He looked at her a long time, then stood back up.

"I'm leaving," he said, walking away.

Montalbano ran after him.

"She was strangled, wasn't she?"

"So it seems."

"How long has she been dead, in your opinion?"

"At least twenty days."

A short while later, Montalbano also decided to leave.

"See you back at the office."

On their way back, Gallo barely missed colliding with a car that was coming fast in the opposite direction.

"They're from TeleVigàta," he said.

Montalbano figured Danzuso had earned his day's pay. He would have sworn on a stack of bibles that he was the one who'd informed the newsmen.

When Fazio returned, Montalbano was just getting up to go and meet Livia in the parking lot.

"What took so long?" the inspector asked.

"We'd just finished when Guarraci arrived, Chief. The guy identified his wife and then fainted. Then he ran away, saying he was gonna go kill himself. To make a long story short, it took a good hour to calm him down."

"Who told him?"

"The TeleVigàta guys. They called him up and told him they were on their way to see a woman's dead body that had just been discovered, and so they thought . . ."

"Okay, okay. What did Forensics say?"

"They confirmed that the body hadn't been at the dump for more than a night."

"The way I see it, the poor lady was seized in the underpass, forced to get into the car that had stopped outside the Via Crocilla exit, taken out to the country, and killed immediately. The corpse was then pulled out and left to be found when Guarraci thought the time was right."

"Chief, the same problem remains: We have no proof."

The phone rang. It was Catarella.

"Chief, 'ere's a jinnelman says 'e wants a talk t'yiz poissonally in poisson."

"What's his name?"

"'E din't say, Chief. 'E jess said as how 'e cou'n't come to p'leece 'eadquatters cuz 'e's layin' in bed."

Montalbano decided to cut things short, had Catarella put him on, and then turned on the speakerphone.

"This is Tano Alletto."

And who was that? He looked at Fazio, who said:

"The night watchman who nearly got run over."

"What can I do for you?" said the inspector.

"Since I gotta high fever, I can't get outta bed, so if you could come here y'sself . . . I got somethin' important to tell you 'bout that goddamn sonofabitch Guarraci."

Montalbano told Livia to go to Calogero's, then dashed off with Fazio to Tano Alletto's house.

4

"Last night, around two a.m., I felt bad and started throwin' up. I realized my temperature was risin'. Maybe it was somethin' I et. An' so I called my son and told him to come to the factory in my place. He arrived half an hour later and I left to come back home. I'd taken about three steps when a car came up really fast an' I was barely able to dodge it. Then I looked at the license plate. It was Guarraci's car. I felt like I was goin' crazy. What, does the guy have it in for me or somethin'? So I started followin' him and saw him take the first road on the left, which goes out to the country. Since it was a dark night, you could see his headlights from far away. The car stopped after about a kilometer and turned off its lights, right around where the Sgarlato brothers live. I wanted to wait for Guarraci to come back so I could bust his face, but I couldn't stand up anymore. Later, when I heard on TV that they found his wife's dead body, I thought I'd better inform you guys."

"You did the right thing," said the inspector. "Are you prepared to repeat what you've just said in court?"

"Absolutely! With all my heart!"

They left Alletto's house.

"Let's go and have a look for ourselves," said Montalbano.

They got into the car and headed for Via Crocilla.

"You know anything about these Sgarlato brothers?"

"Yeah, they're not really people. They're animals. And they live with their sister, who sleeps with both of 'em. They've been arrested and convicted several times for robbery and brawling. They're violent thugs. They've got a vegetable garden, chickens, and rabbits, which is enough for them to live on."

After Via Crocilla, they stopped where the three roads leading into the country began. Alletto was right. At night you could follow a car's headlights a long way.

"There's a good view of the Sgarlato house from here," said Fazio. "It's the first house you cross when you take that road."

"Shall we go?" Montalbano suggested.

"If you say so," Fazio said in resignation.

"Do we have two sets of handcuffs?"

"What do you want to do?"

"I don't know. But let's not waste any time. Have you got a gun for me?"

"No. I can give you mine."

"Lemme have it."

It took them ten minutes to get there. The Sgarlatos' house was not a house but a nasty little two-floor shanty so badly maintained that it was falling apart. It was surrounded by barbed wire and the gate was made of tree branches. Beside the ramshackle structure a large, bottle-green car with only half the rear left fender was parked with its back to the road. It corresponded in every detail with the description given by the witnesses who had seen it drive up Via Crocilla at high speed.

Montalbano and Fazio exchanged a glance. Now they were almost certain that it was the Sgarlato brothers who had kidnapped and murdered Signora Giovanna.

Montalbano started honking the horn. In the doorway appeared a bear whose transformation into a human being hadn't turned out well. He was a mass of beard, hair, and fuzz.

"Got any fresh eggs?" the inspector asked, getting out of the car.

"Yes, I do."

"I'll take a half dozen."

The man went into the house. Fazio got out of the car.

"Get the handcuffs ready," the inspector said to him. "Then gag him and lock him in the car."

The man returned with the eggs wrapped in newspaper.

He handed them to the inspector, who took them. The man was about to open his mouth and tell him how much they cost when Montalbano, smiling, flung the eggs in his face with all his might. And immediately the man found a gun barrel thrust deep into his belly.

"Don't breathe or you're dead."

Fazio handcuffed him. Montalbano hurdled the low fence, ran towards the house, and, once inside, fired a shot into the air.

There was a man and a woman seated at a small table. The man was the twin brother of the bear; the woman a fat, hairy, mustachioed forty-year-old. At one end of the room was a wooden staircase that led to the floor above.

"Stop right where you are and don't say a word!"

Then Fazio, after locking up the bear in the car, arrived and handcuffed the second man as well.

"All right, let me make this perfectly clear," Montalbano then said. "Give me the million lire you took from the purse of the woman you were told to kill, and we won't harm you. But if you don't give it to me we'll kill you both, just like we killed your brother."

Neither of the two said anything.

"I'm sorry, but I have no time to waste," said Montalbano.

With the revolver he gestured to the woman to stand up. She obeyed.

"Go upstairs."

The woman started climbing the stairs. Montalbano followed behind her. They came out in a bedroom consisting of three mattresses on the floor, each beside the other, and three pillows. The stench was unbearable. A den of wild animals would have been less filthy. Clothes strewn about randomly, dirty underwear everywhere. Montalbano bent down, picked up a pair of underpants, and stuffed them into the woman's mouth. Then he tied her hands with whatever he could find. He didn't stop until he figured the woman could no longer move. Then he stuck the barrel of his gun into a pillow and fired one shot. After which he went back downstairs.

"You're the only one left," he said to the bear's twin. "What should we do?"

Despite his beard, the man was visibly pale and scared.

Let's scare him a little more, the inspector thought to himself.

And he fired a shot that passed directly over the man's head. The prisoner fell to his knees.

"Stop! The money's buried in the vegetable garden, in a metal box!"

"Let's go get it," Montalbano said to Sgarlato.

Then, going up to Fazio, he said under his breath:

"You go and find the nearest phone and get some cars and officers here."

Three hours later, following the Sgarlatos' confession, Guarraci, the surveyor, was arrested. Commissioner Burlando covered the inspector's rear by stating that it was he who had authorized them to burst into the killers' house. Livia, on the other hand, raised the roof when Montalbano came home at seven that evening.

"Left alone here for six hours without so much as a phone call!"

After the waters grew calm again, they went out to eat and the inspector made up for missing lunch. When they got back, they sat out on the veranda for a spell, then went to bed. After Livia fell asleep, Montalbano quietly got up and went back out to the veranda to finish the Sciascia novel.

He finished it at three in the morning. But then he stayed up for another hour thinking about it. The story had awakened a suspicion in him. To the point that he slept quite poorly. For this reason, he was already in his office by eight-thirty the next morning.

"Fazio, do you know where Augello can be found?"

"Yeah, Chief. He left the number of a hotel in Taormina."

So the young gent was having a good time of it!

"Ring him and then put me on."

Augello answered in a sleepy voice.

"Mimì, I need you here by four o'clock this afternoon."

"But I'm on sick leave!"

"I don't give a flying fuck. You'll have to leave your leave."

And he hung up. Fazio looked at him in shock.

"I want you here at four, too," the inspector said to him.

That same morning they gave him back his car, all good as new again. And since his ribs hurt only a little, he could drive it.

Augello walked into his office at four o'clock sharp. Fazio was already there.

Mimì was frowning darkly and quite upset. He mumbled a generic greeting and sat down.

"I'd like to know the reason why you felt it necessary to bust my balls and—"

"The reason is that I read a novel."

"And you had me rush all the way here just to tell me that?" said Augello, burning with rage. "You belong in a fucking loony bin!"

"Mimì, I'm telling you for your own good: Calm down and listen to me very carefully. In this novel, a pharmacist receives an anonymous letter containing a death threat to him, and the whole town comes to know about it. Since he doesn't have any enemies, the pharmacist becomes convinced it's just a joke. And one day he goes hunting, as he always does, with his inseparable friend, Dr. Roscio. And both get killed—Roscio surely because he just happened to be there and would have become a dangerous witness. Then at a later point someone discovers that both the anonymous letter and even the murder of the pharmacist were red herrings, in that the real target all along had been Dr. Roscio. Do you like the story?"

"Yes," Augello said drily.

Fazio, for his part, noticed that something in Mimì's demeanor had changed.

"So you're no longer upset that I had you come all the way from Taormina to tell it to you?" asked the inspector.

"Not really," said Augello.

"Well then, Mimì, do you remember the day we were shot at in the car while we were driving? Everyone thought it was me they wanted to kill, whereas that was not the case. When did you, for example, realize this?"

"Not right away."

"When, exactly?"

Augello didn't reply. Then Fazio stood up.

"Chief, you'll have to excuse me," he said, "but I have an important appointment."

"Okay, you can go."

Bravo, Fazio. He'd realized that Augello was having trouble talking with him around. As soon as he went out, Augello said:

"I knew it for certain the day I got home from the hospital."

"What made you so certain?"

"The very same man who shot at me told me."

Montalbano goggled his eyes.

"He came to talk to you?!"

"No, he called me up. In tears."

Montalbano felt more and more at sea.

"And why was he crying?"

"Because he regretted what he'd done, and also because he was happy he hadn't killed or seriously injured anyone with his shots."

"Excuse me for just a minute," said the inspector.

He got up, left the room, and went into the bathroom. He felt as if he was going to explode. He'd turned into a wild beast and wanted to start pummeling Augello. Taking off his shirt, he washed himself all over and went back into his office.

"Tell me everything from the beginning."

"While I was working on the case of the jewel theft, I met

one of the jewelers' wives. A good-looking, honest woman, but . . . I guess I did certain things that made her fall head over heels for me. And so she told me to come to her place one night when her husband was away. The only problem was that he came back much earlier than expected and I was barely able to escape about a minute before he entered the house . . . But he realized just the same what had been happening—his wife's confusion and the unmade bed spoke rather clearly . . . He beat her badly and forced her to tell him my name. And he swore he would kill me. She managed to warn me, that same morning that we were supposed to go and see the commissioner . . . But what could I do?"

"Why didn't you tell me anything?"

"Because you would have acted in accordance with the law and finished off a poor bastard who was already cuckolded and beaten down. And I just didn't feel like it. The whole thing was my fault. But if you decide to press charges for attempted murder and ruin a family, the name of the guy who shot at me is—"

"Don't say it!" the inspector shouted.

And he got up, left the room, and went for a walk in the parking lot, furiously smoking a cigarette. Slowly his rage subsided and he could reason more calmly.

Already hardly anyone was talking about the attempted murder anymore. Another two or three days and it would slip forever under a veil of silence. And it was more than certain that Cusimato's investigation would come to nothing.

He went back to his office. Augello was sitting there bent completely forward, elbows on his knees, head in his hands.

"Go back to Taormina," said the inspector.

Augello shot to his feet and held out his hand.

"Thank you."

The inspector would not shake it.

"Just get the fuck out of here," he ordered him.

DEATH AT SEA

1

It was a spring morning and Montalbano was drinking his customary mug of espresso when the telephone rang. It was Fazio.

"What's up?"

"I got a call from Matteo Cosentino—"

"Sorry, but who's he?"

"Matteo Cosentino is the sole owner of five fishing trawlers."

"And what did he want?"

"He wanted to tell us that there was an accident on one of his boats, the *Carlo III*, in which somebody aboard died."

"What kind of accident?"

"Apparently a crew member inadvertently killed the engineer."

"And where's the boat now?"

"On its way back to Vigàta. It should dock in about forty-five minutes. You can come directly to the port; I'm on my way there now. Should I alert the prosecutor, the forensics lab, and the rest of the crew?"

"Let's check out the situation first."

As he was heading for Vigàta he wondered what mysterious reason Cosentino could have had for naming his fishing boat after a Spanish king, but couldn't think of an answer. The area reserved for trawlers was at the far end of the central jetty, where there was a long row of refrigerated warehouses. It wasn't yet time for the boats to return from their fishing runs, and so there were few people about.

Montalbano spotted the squad car and pulled up beside it. Fazio was a short way off, talking to a squat, shabby-looking man of about sixty.

Fazio introduced them. Matteo Cosentino immediately explained to the inspector that his fishing boat was late because it had engine problems.

"How did you learn of the accident?"

"From the ship's radio. The crew chief called me at three o'clock in the morning."

"And what time was it when you called the police?"

"Seven."

"Why did you wait so long?"

"Inspector, the whole thing happened five hours out at sea from here. If I called you right away, what were you gonna do? Get on a boat and join them out on the open sea?"

"Did the crew chief tell you how the accident happened?"

"He summed it up for me."

"Well, then sum it up for me, too."

"The ship's mechanic, whose name is Franco Arnone, was in the motor compartment working on some malfunction, and Tano Cipolla, a crew member, was sitting on the edge of the hatch and talking to him as he was cleaning his pistol, when—"

"Wait a second. Are the crews of your trawlers armed?"

"Not that I know of."

"So how do you explain that Cipolla had a pistol?"

"How should I know? You can ask him when they get here."

"There's a trawler coming in," Fazio announced.

Matteo looked out towards the harbor entrance.

"It's the *Carlo III*," he confirmed.

Montalbano couldn't hold back his curiosity.

"I'm sorry, but why did you give your boat that name?"

"All my fishing boats are called *Carlo* and go from one to five. In memory of my only son, who died when he was twenty."

As the trawler was docking, a number of idlers approached, curious at the boat's unscheduled reentry.

Once they learned there was a corpse aboard, the crowd would swell to a hundred or more and create tremendous confusion, making it difficult to work. Montalbano made a snap decision and turned to speak to Cosentino.

"Don't let any of the crew disembark. The three of us will go aboard, and then I want the boat to put out again."

"And where should I tell them to go?" asked Cosentino.

"Right outside the harbor will be enough for me. Then they can stop wherever they want."

Ten minutes later the boat was rocking, engines off, about half a kilometer from the lighthouse that was the destination of Montalbano's daily digestive walks. From the bridge, looking through the hatch to the engine compartment, one got a good view of the body of the man who'd been killed. He was in a strange position, kneeling in front of the engine, his right arm raised, held up by a handle in which his hand had become entangled. The back of his head was gone, the walls of the compartment stuck with scattered fragments of bone and brain matter.

"Which one of you is Tano Cipolla?"

One man stepped away from the group of sailors standing astern and talking to Cosentino, a very lean forty-year-old, pale and agitated, wild-eyed, hair standing on end. He moved in fits and starts, like a mechanical puppet.

"It was a terrible mistake! I was just—"

"You can tell me that later. Now go to the exact spot where you were when you shot the mechanic."

Cipolla protested. His voice was quavering, his eyes on the verge of tears.

"But I didn't mean to shoot Franco!"

"Okay. But, in the meantime, just show me."

Still like a puppet, Tano Cipolla sat down on the edge of the hatch with his legs dangling into the motor room.

"This is exactly how I was. And I was talking to him while he worked."

"Did you already have your gun in your hand?"

"No, sir."

"Weren't you cleaning it?"

"Who ever said that?"

At this point Fazio intervened.

"Give me your weapon."

"I ain't got it anymore. As soon as I realized I'd killed Franco, I threw it into the sea."

"Why?"

"I dunno. You can't understand. I was desperate, I was mad . . ."

"What kind of gun was it?"

"A Colt revolver."

"What caliber?"

"Dunno."

"Do you have extra cartridges?"

"Yessir, about thirty. They're in my bag."

"Where did you buy it?"

Cipolla became tongue-tied.

"I got . . . I got it from a friend."

"Did you register it?"

"No, sir."

"Do you have a license to bear arms?"

"No, sir."

"Are you done yet?" Fazio asked the inspector.

"For now, yes."

"So I'll repeat my question: Why at some point did you take out your gun?"

"He asked me to."

"Explain."

"I'd told him I owned a gun, and so he asked to see it."

"I see. And where did you have it at that moment?"

"In my bag."

"What did you do?"

"I got up, went and got the gun, and then sat back down. And that was when . . ."

"When what?"

"When it went off. We took a wave across the deck, and to keep from falling into the engine compartment, I grabbed the edge with both hands. And without realizing it I probably squeezed the trigger too tight, and . . ."

"Okay. Stand up. Fazio, please give the gentleman your pistol."

Fazio didn't really feel like it, but he gave it to him anyway, after removing the cartridge clip.

"Now, Signor Cipolla, I want you to repeat the movements you made, and you should even pull the trigger when the moment comes."

Everyone on board watched the scene. Cipolla sat down and, as soon as he was seated, lurched suddenly chest-forward, spread his arms, grabbed the edge of the hatch with both hands at his sides, and at that moment they all heard the click of the pistol's hammer striking an empty chamber.

It was a plausible reconstruction. The accident could, in fact, have happened that way.

"Give Signor Fazio back his gun and remain seated."

The inspector then turned to the rest of the crew.

"Did you all hear the shot?"

There was a chorus of yeses.

"What were you all doing at that moment?"

The sailors looked at one another, a little confused, and didn't answer.

"Can I speak for everyone?" asked a sandy-haired man of about fifty with sun-baked skin and a Phoenician face.

"And who are you?"

"I'm the crew chief, Angelo Sidoti."

"All right, speak."

"The pilot was at the helm, four men were astern checking the nets, and I was walking from stern to prow to—"

"So you were the person closest to the spot where—"

"Yessir, I was."

"What did you do?"

"I took two steps back and realized immediately what had happened. Cipolla was frozen like a statue with a gun in its hand. I looked into the engine room and didn't take long to figure out that poor Franco was dead."

"Then what did you do?"

"I rushed over to the radio to call Signor Cosentino."

"And then?"

"Then I informed the other boats that we were suspending the fishing expedition and heading back to Vigàta. And then I heard some shouting and so I went out on deck."

"Who was yelling?"

"Cipolla. It was like he'd gone crazy. Girolamo and Nicola were restraining him, 'cause he wanted to throw himself into the sea."

Montalbano walked away towards the prow and called Fazio over.

"Listen, I want Cosentino, Cipolla, and the crew chief in my office at four o'clock this afternoon. And everyone else should remain available. As soon as we get back, inform the prosecutor, Pasquano, and Forensics. I'm going back to the office. Tell Cosentino we can return to port."

After the inspector had been signing papers for an hour, Augello came in. He'd been in bed for four days with the flu.

"How are you feeling?"

"Fully recovered," said Augello, sitting down. "I heard there was an accident out on a fishing boat."

"Yeah, some fisherman, one Tano Cipolla, accidentally shot the engine man . . ."

"What did you say the shooter's name was?"

"Cipolla. Tano Cipolla."

"Cipolla . . . Tano Cipolla . . . Want to bet he's the guy married to the two twins?" Augello asked himself aloud.

"What the hell are you talking about?"

"There's a pair of twin girls here in Vigàta, Lella and Lalla, famous for their beauty, who are now around thirty years old."

"Are you kidding me?"

"No. Lella married Cipolla, and Lalla remained unmarried but lives with her sister and brother-in-law. Around town they call him the twins' husband."

"But how do you know these things?"

"I know everything about the beautiful women of Vigàta," Augello said with a grin.

Montalbano realized that grin was hiding something.

"Don't tell me you tried your luck with them!"

"No, I never did. But I later regretted it, when I started to hear rumors."

"Saying what?"

"Saying that on certain nights, when Cipolla is away, his wife entertains. Not often, but sometimes."

"And what does Lalla do in the meantime?"

"Well, she certainly doesn't sit in her room twiddling her thumbs. She takes part. They do threesomes. But these are just rumors. There may be nothing to them."

"And does Cipolla know anything about these escapades of his wife and sister-in-law?"

"There are some who are convinced Cipolla's in the dark

about the whole thing, and then others who swear Cipolla knows everything but pretends not to know anything."

"Do me a favor, Mimì, and try to get more information."

"Why, do you have doubts about the accident?"

"For the moment, no, but it's always best to be aware of all the possibilities."

2

By the time Fazio returned, the inspector was already about to go out to eat.

"What took so long?"

"Dr. Pasquano made a wrong move trying to turn his car around and ended up with both front wheels hanging off the pier, looking like some balancing act at the circus. He very nearly plunged straight into the water."

"What did he say?"

"He was cursing like a madman. Scared to death."

"No, I meant what did he say about the corpse?"

"He said the man died instantly and that it must have happened between two and four a.m. last night."

"That fits."

"Right. Forensics found the bullet. It was pretty misshapen. They'll keep us posted."

As he was eating some exquisite mullet *al cartoccio*, the inspector thought of something and called Calogero, the owner, over to his table.

"What is it, Inspector?"

"Tell me something. Where do you buy your fish?"

"From Felice Sorrentino."

"And have you ever used Matteo Cosentino?"

"I did, for a while. But then I switched."

"Why?"

"Because twice he tried to pull a fast one on me."

"How?"

"By selling me frozen fish he was passing off as fresh."

"Apparently he hadn't caught enough to allow him—"

"People say it happens often. His boats come back half-empty, and since he doesn't want to lose customers, he buys frozen fish from some of his colleagues."

"But has he always done that?"

"He was dependable at first. The problems started about three or four years ago."

A walk out to the lighthouse was in order. Sitting down on the flat rock, he fired up a cigarette. After what Mimì Augello had told him, he realized they had to leave no stone unturned in their interrogation of Cipolla. He looked at his watch: three o'clock.

He sat there a little while longer, breathing the sea air deep into his lungs. When he got back to the station, Fazio informed him that those summoned were already there.

"Let's start with the crew chief. What's his name again?"

"Angelo Sidoti."

"What do you know about him?"

"He's fifty-one, has always worked for Cosentino, and is top dog among all the other crew chiefs."

"What's that mean?"

"It means that if a dangerous situation arises, he's the boss and everyone has to follow his orders."

The inspector sat Sidoti down in the chair opposite his desk. Sidoti seemed neither nervous nor worried; in fact, his attitude seemed almost indifferent.

"Signor Sidoti, you told me where you were when the shot went off. Where were you five minutes before that?"

The crew chief answered at once.

"Five minutes before that, I was in the wheelhouse."

"So, if I've understood correctly, you went from the wheelhouse to the stern, where four crewmen were checking the nets, you engaged them briefly, and were on your way back to the wheelhouse when you were stopped by the shot?"

"That's correct."

"Where did Cipolla keep his knapsack?"

"There's a space on the prow where we can store our things."

"So—please correct me if I'm wrong—to go and get his gun, Cipolla in fact had to travel from near the stern to a spot near the prow, thus covering almost the entire length of the boat. Is that right?"

"Yes, that's right."

"Now pay close attention. When you came out of the wheelhouse and went astern, did you see Cipolla sitting on the edge of the hatch opening?"

This time, too, Sidoti answered without hesitation.

"No, he wasn't there."

"How can you be so sure? It was the middle of the night and—"

"Inspector, we make do just fine with the navigation lights; we're used to it. Apparently he'd gone to get his gun."

"So then you must have seen him return."

"Yes, that I did. We crossed paths outside the engine compartment. Then I took two more steps and heard the shot, at which point I turned around and saw what I already told you."

"When you crossed paths with Cipolla, did you notice he was holding a gun?"

"No."

"How long has Cipolla been working with you?"

"That was his first time aboard my boat."

This answer took Montalbano by surprise.

"Where was he before that?"

"On the *Carlo I*."

"Why was he moved?"

"Those are things Signor Cosentino decides."

"Was it also the first time aboard for the engine mechanic?"

"No, he's been working for me for three years."

"I'm sure you've discussed what happened with your men. Did anyone overhear what Cipolla and Arnone were talking about before the shot was fired?"

"The guys checking the nets were about ten feet away from the engine room and shooting the breeze. It's unlikely they heard anything."

"Did Cipolla and Arnone already know each other?"

"Of course. Since we all work for the same boss, we all know each other."

"Thank you. You can go now."

Sidoti said good-bye and left. Fazio and the inspector exchanged a glance.

"What do you think?" asked Fazio.

"To tell you the truth, I'm not convinced. He was too ready with his answers."

"Explain what you mean."

"How is it possible for someone to remember immediately everything he did, minute by minute, the night before? A lot of it was habitual acts and gestures he must have done hundreds of times, and you're gonna remember exactly where you were at an exact given moment?"

"Maybe in the meantime he'd gone over those moments in his mind."

"I'm sure that's true. Have Signor Cosentino come in."

Signor Cosentino appeared immediately, more nervous than that morning.

"I was told my trawler will be under a restraining order for at least a week. I'm going to lose a ton of money!"

Montalbano pretended not to have heard him.

"Signor Sidoti has just told us that Cipolla was on his first fishing expedition aboard the *Carlo III*, after working on the *Carlo I*, and that he was moved there on your orders."

"So what? Ain't I got the right to move one of my fishermen from one boat to another?"

"Of course you do, but you'll have to tell me the reason."

"Mr. Inspector, it just happens sometimes that when certain people spend too much time on the same boat with each other, they end up getting on each other's nerves. And that's when the arguments and scuffles start . . . and the work suffers."

"Had you received any complaints?"

"Complaints, no, but I got a good nose for certain things."

"So has your nose sniffed out anything else?"

"What do you mean?"

"I'm told that Cipolla has a beautiful wife and that his sister-in-law, who lives with them, is also no joke."

"Would you please come right out and say what you're getting at?"

"Was Arnone married?"

"No, sir. He was a good-looking kid of about thirty and a real ladies' man."

"Okay, now you're talking. Is it possible Cipolla may have heard some nasty rumors about his wife and Arnone?"

Cosentino threw up his hands in a gesture of surrender.

"Anything's possible," he said.

"We need to find out whether Arnone knew Signora Cipolla."

"I can answer that question myself. He most certainly did know her."

"How do you know?"

"Because every New Year's Eve, I invite all my crews with their families to my house. But if you want to know what I think—"

"Tell me."

"If Cipolla really intended to kill Arnone, couldn't he have found a better place to do it? To kill a man like that, on a fishing boat, in front of everyone . . ."

"Okay, that'll be enough for today. Fazio, please bring in Signor Cipolla."

Apparently Cipolla had had all the time in the world to

calm himself down. He was no longer wild-eyed, and had meanwhile combed his hair. He even seemed more sure of himself, and the questions they asked would no longer catch him unprepared. As soon as he appeared before him, Montalbano realized instinctively that the best strategy would be to make him all nervous again, as he was that morning. And so he immediately went on the attack.

"Signor Cipolla, aside from the fact that you're up against the very serious charge of murder—"

"What the fuck are you talking about?! Murder?!" Cipolla immediately interrupted him.

The inspector slammed his hand down on the desk and raised his voice, surprising Fazio, who looked at him in shock.

"Don't you ever dare interrupt me! You will listen to me in silence, and if I ask you to speak, you will use proper language! And be careful what you say. I'll only tell you this once. Do we understand each other?"

"Yes, sir," said a frightened Cipolla.

"And I will add, for your information, that if it had been up to me, I would have arrested you already, but His Honor the judge did not agree, and I must therefore keep interrogating you."

Cipolla's brow quickly became drenched in sweat.

"Now, in addition to homicide charges, you will have to answer for illegal possession of a firearm. Is that clear?"

"Yes."

"For what reason, in your opinion, did Signor Cosentino take you off of the *Carlo I* and transfer you to the *Carlo III*?"

"How should I know ? . . . He's the boss . . ."

"Don't waste my time, Cipolla. And don't try to get cute

with me. Cosentino told me everything. Will it make it easier for you if I tell you the reason myself?"

Cipolla, resigned, threw up his hands and said nothing.

"You," Montalbano continued, "weren't getting along with your mates on the *Carlo I* anymore. And do you want me to tell you why? Your wife—"

All at once Cipolla shot to his feet, red in the face and trembling.

"Leave my wife out of this!"

Fazio grabbed him by the arm, put the other hand on his shoulder, and forced him to sit back down.

"It's all lies! Malicious gossip based on nothing!" a very upset Cipolla said through clenched teeth.

"Try to calm down and, for your own good, think carefully before you answer my questions. Were you a friend of Franco Arnone?"

Cipolla took a deep breath before answering.

"Friend, no. An acquaintance."

"Now try to answer me without making a scene, otherwise I'll have you thrown in a holding cell. Did Arnone and your wife know each other?"

"Of course. Franco knew Lella before she became my wife."

"Tell me more."

"Franco was head over heels in love with Lalla, my wife's twin sister. Lalla went along at first, but then she left him."

"I'm beginning to understand," said the inspector.

And he cast a quick glance over at Fazio, which meant for him to be ready to intervene. Fazio nudged himself to the edge of his seat.

3

"I understand," Montalbano repeated pensively.

And he said no more. The silence grew heavy. Cipolla started to get nervous, then couldn't hold back any longer.

"Could you tell me . . ."

"Absolutely. I'm convinced that Arnone wanted compensation from your wife for Lalla's rejection, and that he got it."

At first Cipolla didn't understand. Then the meaning of the inspector's words began to sink in. With a kind of roar he shot to his feet and flew over the top of the desk at Montalbano before Fazio could restrain him. But the inspector had stood up and stepped aside, so that Cipolla ended his flight by crashing his head against the wall and collapsing to the floor, stunned. Fazio helped him back up, sat him down again, and brought him a glass of water.

"Sorry about that," Cipolla said moments later, still breathing heavily.

A change had come over him. Maybe he'd realized that it was best to keep his nerves in check.

"Can I continue?"

"Yessir."

"You know what led me to make that conjecture? The fact that you, before boarding the *Carlo III*, had a friend give you a revolver and—"

"But I'd had the gun already for a while!"

"But you can't prove that."

Cipolla closed his eyes and threw his head back. He was starting to feel lost.

"Then, if you'd already had it for a while, my question is: Were you also armed when you worked aboard the *Carlo I*?"

"Yessir, I was."

"Can you explain to me why?"

"I can explain, but I wouldn't want the others to know that I explained it to you."

"What have the others got to do with it?"

"Well, they . . . Okay, I'll tell you the whole story and get it over with . . . It's because sometimes, while we're fishing, some patrol boats from Libya, Tunisia, an' who knows where the hell else, arrive out of nowhere and hijack some of our boats. An' I don't feel like ending up in one of Gaddafi's prisons."

"Has that already happened to you?"

"Not to me personally, but to a friend o' mine, yes. And he told me they did shameful things to him."

"So your gun was for self-defense?"

"Of course."

"But what could you have done all alone against the machine guns of a patrol boat?"

Cipolla said nothing.

"As you can see, your explanation doesn't hold water. And, I must warn you, your situation is looking worse and worse. We're actually moving towards a charge of premeditated murder, so you'd better forget about your 'accident' claim. Anyway, now I'm going to call the investigating judge and—"

"Wait a second," Cipolla said softly.

He was wringing his hands and rocking his upper body back and forth in his chair. Montalbano prodded him a little.

"Okay, that's enough."

"Whoever said I was the only one with a weapon?" Cipolla cried out.

"Just a minute, let me get this straight. Are you telling me your fellow crewmen were also armed?"

"Yes, I am."

"Do you think your mates are ready to confirm that for me?"

"Not in my wildest dreams."

"Why not?"

"First of all because they don't have gun permits, and secondly because I'm the one who screwed up, and so I have to pay."

Suddenly, upon hearing these last replies, a little light came on inside the inspector's brain.

"So, maybe, aboard the boat, there was something bigger than a revolver?"

"I ain't no snitch."

The little light grew brighter.

"Is Signor Cosentino aware of this?"

Cipolla shrugged.

"Maybe, maybe not. He's got his own reasons for not wanting his boat hijacked."

Silence fell. Then Montalbano asked:

"You realize that, as things stand now, you're fucked?"

Cipolla hung his head down to his chest and started silently weeping.

"I swear I didn't wanna kill him! It was an accident!"

"Unfortunately for you, however . . ."

A kind of wail began to come out of Cipolla's mouth.

Montalbano decided the moment had come to deliver the decisive blow. He'd given him the bitter part; now he would give him the sweet. He spoke in a soft voice.

". . . Though I, personally, am beginning to have serious doubts as to the premeditation."

As Cipolla's body shook as if from a jolt of electricity, Fazio smiled. He'd grasped the inspector's game.

"So you believe me?" a disoriented Cipolla asked, incredulous.

"I might. But I need to ask a few more questions."

"Whatever you like."

"And you must answer me with the utmost sincerity."

"I swear I will."

"So you confirm for me that your mates were also armed?"

"Yessir."

"And the engine man likewise?"

"Yessir."

"Where'd he keep his weapon?"

"In his waistband."

"You threw your own weapon into the sea after the accident, but when did your mates get rid of theirs?"

"After Sidoti told them to."

"And was Sidoti acting under orders from Cosentino?"

"I don't know whether or not Cosentino gave the order, but in any case Sidoti told us after talking to him."

"What else did Sidoti throw into the sea?"

Cipolla hesitated slightly for a moment. Montalbano decided to intervene.

"Signor Cipolla, you have two roads before you: on the one hand, thirty years for premeditated murder, and on the

other, a few short years for manslaughter and illegal possession of a handgun. The decision is yours. I repeat: What else
did Sidoti throw into the sea?"

"A . . . a Kalashnikov."

Montalbano immediately realized that Cipolla was hiding
something else.

"And in addition to the Kalashnikov?"

"Two wet suits, two diving masks, and four oxygen
tanks," Cipolla said under his breath.

"What were they used for?"

Before answering, Cipolla furrowed his brow as though
it cost him great effort.

"To . . . to disentangle the net, if necess—"

"I'm sorry, but then what need was there to get rid of
them?"

"I don't know."

It was clear the guy was lying, but the inspector chose not
to press the point.

"Are the crews of the other trawlers also armed?"

"Yessir."

Then Fazio spoke.

"When they pulled the mechanic's body out, there was
no weapon."

"Sidoti had gone down into the engine room and taken
it," said Cipolla.

"That'll be all for now," said the inspector. "Fazio, take
him to a holding cell. You're under arrest, Signor Cipolla."

Cipolla, who hadn't expected this outcome, sat there in
shock, mouth open, lacking even the strength to stand up.
Fazio helped him to his feet and dragged him along. Five
minutes later he hurried back and sat down.

"But what do you really think about Cipolla?" he asked the inspector.

"I'm beginning to become convinced that it actually was an accident, but one that produced undesirable results."

"What does that mean?"

"It means that this little killing is endangering some shady activity the nature of which I have yet to discover. We need to find out more about Cosentino."

"Already taken care of," said Fazio.

Every time Fazio said "already taken care of," which he did often, it meant he was one step ahead of him, something that made the inspector feel tremendously annoyed. But he controlled himself.

"Who'd you talk to?"

"To my dad. I went to see him after lunch, before coming here."

"And what did he tell you?"

Fazio beamed, as if on a grand occasion.

"My father told me some interesting things. Many years ago, Cosentino was a poor wretch of a fisherman whom Don Ramunno Cuffaro—"

"Ay-yai-yai . . ." said Montalbano.

". . . whom Don Ramunno Cuffaro took under his wing, to the point that he made him crew chief of a special fishing boat."

"What was so special about it?"

"Aside from fishing for fish, it also fished for contraband cigarettes."

"I get it. So he made his career with the Cuffaros?"

"Exactly. My father is convinced that he's not the real owner of those trawlers, but just a front man for the Cuffaros."

"Anything else?"

"Yeah. They say his son Carlo, who officially drowned at sea six years ago and whose body was never recovered, was actually killed in a shoot-out with the Sinagras, who'd sent out two trawlers to steal the Cuffaros' cigarettes. At that point, apparently, Cosentino got the Cuffaros to allow him to work solely as an honest fisherman, whereas now——"

"Whereas now he's been called back into service. But what kind of service? That's the question. Listen, do you know any trawler owners who are honest and discreet?"

"Yes. Calogero Lorusso."

"Turn on the speakerphone, give him a ring, and then put me on."

Five minutes later he had Lorusso on the phone.

"What can I do for you, Inspector?"

"I would ask you to keep our conversation to yourself."

"I'm as silent as the grave."

"Thank you. I'd like to know what sort of instructions you give your crews in the event a foreign patrol boat should attempt to sequester them."

"Well, Inspector, the instructions aren't mine. All Italian fishing boats are supposed to abide by the rules issued by the Harbormasters' Central Command."

"And what would they be?"

"First of all, to try to avoid sequester by moving away at maximum speed, even if it means abandoning our nets. Second, not to put up any resistance, not even in the face of serious provocation. Third, not to carry any weapons whatsoever on board. Fourth——"

"That's enough, thanks. But tell me something. If your nets get stuck, do you send a diver down?"

"A diver? At night? Are you kidding? We just try and try with the capstan, hoping that with the right maneuver and a little luck . . ."

"One last question, then I'll let you go. How are the fisheries divided up between you and your colleagues?"

"There's nothing in writing. It's just the traditional fisheries. If we were on land, you could call it acquisitive prescription. I've had my own area for decades, Filipoti's got his, Cosentino likewise, and so on."

"Thank you for your help."

Montalbano hung up and dialed another number with his eyes on a piece of paper in front of him.

"Signor Cosentino, Montalbano here. I wanted to inform you that Cipolla's under arrest, so you could let his wife know. Tomorrow morning he'll be transferred to Montelusa prison. I'll be reporting to the judge that in my opinion we're dealing with premeditated murder."

"So when can I have my trawler back?"

"I'll ask the judge to lift the restraining order, first thing tomorrow morning. Have a good evening."

He hung up and looked over at Fazio.

"That way, Cosentino will feel safe to keep doing what he does. Because there's no doubt he's doing something shady, considering that he's breaking the Harbormasters' rules."

"His trawlers are so heavily armed they might as well be a naval squadron," said Fazio.

"Exactly. My dear Fazio, I'm under the impression we're looking at something big. But it's getting late now, so I'm going to head on home. One thing, however: I want you to find out where Cosentino's fishing area is located. See you in the morning."

When he got home he realized he didn't feel like doing anything, not even eating.

There was a question swirling about in his head: What was Cosentino's secret?

And the fact that he couldn't answer it weighed heavily on him.

He decided to have a little snack, just so he wouldn't go to bed on an empty stomach.

4

He prepared a platter of salami, caciocavallo cheese, prosciutto, and ten or so passuluna olives, then grabbed a bottle of wine and brought everything out onto the veranda. This kept him busy for about an hour, after which he went back inside and turned on the television. They were broadcasting the third installment of *La Piovra*, a TV series on the Mafia that was enjoying tremendous success. He watched it for a bit. It was as though the Italians had only just discovered Sicily, but only for its worst side, and so he changed the channel. And he found Toto Cutugno singing "*Con la chitarra in mano,*" from "L' Italiano," which he'd presented at the San Remo festival the year before. He turned off the set and went back out to the veranda to smoke and rack his brain. At that hour the fishing boats of Vigàta were heading out towards their respective fishing zones.

But what did Cosentino's boats fish?

Finally, around midnight, it was time to phone Livia.

She said she'd just got back from the movies.

"What did you see?"

"A double-oh-seven movie with James Bond."

"But those are spy fables!"

"And in fact I saw it as a fable. Totally unreal. Just think, at a certain point they hide an airplane at the bottom of the sea, covering it with a tarp, then they send some frogmen down to the plane to recover some . . ."

But Montalbano, following his own thoughts, was no longer listening . . .

"Thanks," he blurted out at one point.

"Thanks for what?" asked Livia, confused.

Montalbano set her straight.

"Thanks for telling me the plot of the film. That way I don't have to go and see it."

"But I wasn't talking about the film anymore! I was telling you I really feel like being with you, and you come out and say 'thanks' like I was offering you a cigarette! Go to hell!"

And she hung up angrily. Montalbano called back and needed a good ten minutes to make peace.

But when he lay down in bed, he didn't fall asleep right away. Livia's words had been like a ray of light that illuminates a dark corner for a few seconds, allowing you a momentary glimpse of what's there . . .

And thus he was able, after jumping from hypothesis to hypothesis, to arrive at a possible conclusion. One truly worthy of a James Bond movie.

"I've got some good information," Fazio said cheerfully the following morning, when entering the office. "I had a long talk with Calogero Lorusso. Cosentino's fishery is just opposite the Gulf of Sirte, but still in our territorial waters, a seven-hour sail from Vigàta. The area is called the 'shallows of Ghabuz' because the water's not very deep around there."

"Shallow water? Just the words I wanted to hear."

"Lorusso also told me about something strange he'd noticed."

"What?"

"That Cosentino's five boats always put out together, but every fifteenth day one of the boats returns some three or four hours later than the others. And this has been going on for the past few years. He also said that if I wanted to check, all I have to do is go to the harbor tomorrow, because tomorrow's the fifteenth day."

"All right, then. I'm going now to see the judge in Montelusa about Cipolla's arrest and to lift the restraining order on Cosentino's boat. I'll be back in two hours at the most. You, in the meantime, should try to find out where the radio that Cosentino uses to communicate with his boats is located. Look carefully as to where the doors and windows are."

"What have you got in mind?" Fazio asked suspiciously.

"I'll tell you later."

He convinced the judge that Cipolla should remain in detention despite the fact that he himself was almost certain that the killing was a case of involuntary manslaughter; he obtained a signed order lifting the sequestration; and from the phone in the courthouse he informed Cosentino of the news, telling him he could drop by to pick up the document around one p.m., but in the meantime he could remove the seals and get the boat ready to sail. Cosentino thanked him endlessly.

When he got back he left the order lifting the sequestration with Catarella and found Fazio waiting for him in his office.

"Before anything else, you must answer a question: At what time do Cosentino's boats put out?"

"At two p.m."

"So they should reach their fishery by nine, fish until midnight, then return home, getting to the port of Vigàta around seven in the morning, correct?"

"Correct."

"Now it's your turn to talk."

"Cosentino's office is on the road that runs along the edge of the port, at number twenty-two. It's in a warehouse where they store spare parts and fishing nets. The actual office consists of a sort of loft that you reach by way of a narrow iron staircase. That's where he's got his radio. There's also a bed, because sometimes Cosentino spends the night there."

"I'd bet the family jewels he's going to spend the night there tonight. How can I get in there?"

"Without authorization?"

"Good guess."

"Chief, you must know that this could turn out badly for you."

"Answer my question."

"In back there's a window that's always half-open. But if you go, Chief, I'm going with you."

"No. At the most you can stay outside and be my lookout. I want you to post a guard outside the warehouse starting at seven o'clock tonight. As soon as Cosentino returns, you must inform me at home. Now go get Augello and come back."

When Mimì arrived, the inspector told him the conclusions he'd drawn and the plan he had in mind.

"Just one observation," Mimì said when he'd finished. "You haven't the slightest idea what crime Cosentino and his men are committing. And, I'm sorry, but that's not much to go on."

"Mimì, what's certain is that they *are* committing a crime. What kind of crime, we won't find out until we get our hands on those fishing boats. It'll be like the surprise inside an Easter egg."

━━━━━

Fazio's call came in at eight, and at eight-thirty the inspector was pulling up behind Cosentino's warehouse in a deserted alley. Before getting out, he took his pistol from the glove compartment and put it in his jacket pocket. Fazio was waiting for him.

"Cosentino is inside and has locked the main door. This is the window here. It's open enough to get through. I'll give you a hand. Climb up onto my shoulders."

A moment later the inspector was sitting on the windowsill. Then he turned around and, grabbing onto the edge, slid down noiselessly.

He was inside. The light was on. He could hear Cosentino talking to someone on the phone. Montalbano stood there and looked around. The warehouse wasn't very big, but it was stuffed with crates, engine parts, and fishing nets. The loft area where Cosentino had his office was made of masonry and attached to the wall on the left-hand side of the building.

It had a window that gave onto the interior of the warehouse. Montalbano was convinced that Cosentino wouldn't be able to see him unless he looked out that window. Under the loft there were more crates, and the inspector decided that was the best place to go and hide. Cosentino was still talking over the phone. Montalbano moved very slowly and with great care. Finally, with a sigh he wedged himself between two crates. As soon as Cosentino had finished talking, a voice came over the radio.

"*Carlo III* to home base. *Carlo III* to home base."

The voice was Sidoti's.

"I hear you, *Carlo III.*"

"We're at Ghabuz. Should all five of us start fishing?"

"For the moment, yes."

What did that "for the moment" mean? That Cosentino was awaiting orders?

This was going to take a while. Moving very slowly, Montalbano managed to sit down on the ground with his back against the wall. He heard Cosentino get up and was afraid he would come downstairs. Moments later, however, Cosentino sat back down. Every so often he heard him humming a tune. Ever so slowly, a dangerous sleepiness started to come over him. He defended himself by reciting in his mind whatever he could remember from the *Orlando Furioso*, and then *The Iliad*. He didn't know how much time had passed. Then he heard Cosentino's telephone ring. The man said: "Hello?" and then listened in silence. In the end he said, "Okay," and hung up. A moment later he spoke over the radio.

"Home base to *Carlo III*. Home base to *Carlo III.*"

"*Carlo III* here, over. What's the order?"

"Pass the position I gave you over to Taibi; the *Carlo II*'s gonna pick up the stuff. When Taibi tells you he's arrived, give me a call. It should take about an hour. Your four other boats should keep on trawling."

More time passed. Then Sidoti's voice returned.

"*Carlo III* to home base."

"Home base here, go ahead."

"Taibi informs me the *Carlo II* is at the buoy and starting the operation. He says he should be able to do it in half an hour."

"Okay, I'll hail you in a few minutes to give you the instructions for Taibi."

Amidst the great silence the inspector distinctly heard Cosentino dialing a telephone number. Then he heard:

"Hello? They've started the retrieval. I want to know what my trawler's supposed to do with the stuff."

As Cosentino was listening to the answer, Montalbano stood up, took out his pistol, reached the foot of the iron staircase in a flash, and started climbing gingerly. Cosentino, sitting at a table with a radio and telephone on it, had his back to him.

"All right," said Cosentino, putting down the receiver.

And at that moment he felt a gun barrel press against the back of his neck. He froze.

"Turn around."

Cosentino turned, remaining seated, and as soon as he recognized Montalbano, his mouth dropped and stayed open.

"Now listen closely. Nobody on the police force knows I'm here. So I can shoot and kill you and nobody would be any the wiser. After they find your body, I'll be the one doing the investigation and I'll blame the Sinagras. So you can consider yourself a dead man. Do you understand what I'm saying?"

Cosentino nodded in affirmation. He was drooling, the saliva dripping from the corners of his mouth.

"Now, I'm going to ask you a question, and if you don't answer it to my satisfaction, I'll shoot you in the knee. And if you still don't answer, I'll shoot your other knee. And I'll keep on going until you make up your mind."

Cosentino had turned a greenish hue.

"What instructions were you given for the *Carlo II*?"

"It's . . . supposed to . . . stay close . . . to the buoy . . . which . . . a motorboat . . . 'll be there . . . in about an hour and . . ."

"And now you're going to tell them the orders have changed and that the *Carlo II* should join the other four boats and they should all sail back to Vigàta. And they should put the stuff they picked up in the forehold. Now, you need to calm down before talking over the radio. Your voice has to sound the way it always does."

Cosentino obeyed.

"Just out of curiosity, could you tell me what you retrieved from the bottom of the sea?"

Cosentino opened his eyes wide in surprise.

"You didn't know?"

"No."

"Thirty kilos of heroin."

He escorted Cosentino out of the warehouse. Fazio came running as soon as he saw them.

"Have the reinforcements from Montelusa arrived?"

"Yessir."

"Then inform Inspector Augello that the five trawlers are returning to port and that in the forehold of the *Carlo II* he'll find thirty kilos of heroin. Arrest all the crewmen; they're armed and dangerous. And I'm turning Signor Cosentino over to you. Take him and put him in a holding cell."

"And what are you going to do?"

"I'm going home to bed. I'm a little tired."

He'd just spent a nasty afternoon fending off journalists wanting interviews when he had to dash off to Montelusa to receive first a tongue-lashing and then praise from the commissioner. After that he was summoned by the judge to explain everything. But he sang him only half the Mass.

He got home at nine that evening, agitated and tired. But he had a good sleep, and showed up at the office the next morning in a good mood.

"I need to talk to you," said Mimì Augello, coming into his office.

"So talk."

"Did you tell the judge you think Cipolla was guilty of involuntary manslaughter?"

"I'm convinced he is."

"You're wrong. I have two witnesses. Over the past month, Arnone'd been going at night to Cipolla's house when he wasn't there."

Montalbano thought about this for a moment.

"You know what I say to you, Mimì? Never mind about the judge. He'll decide for himself. In my opinion, Cipolla deserves a little help."

THE STOLEN MESSAGE

1

It was too late. He'd already half undressed and gone and sat
on the veranda to smoke a last cigarette when he realized he
no longer had so much as a drop of whisky in the house. Not
that he wanted it so badly, of course. He would have been
happy with just a finger's worth, but the utter lack of it in-
creased his desire.

He tried to resist. What was he, an alcoholic or something? And yet, without the whisky, the cigarette he was
smoking tasted downright insipid. In the end he couldn't
stand it any longer.

Cursing the saints, he threw on some clothes as best he
could, left the house, got in the car, and headed towards the
bar outside of Marinella. But he'd forgotten that on Sundays
it closed at nine, and so he had to continue on to Vigàta, as
far as the Caffè Castiglione.

As he was about to enter, a portly man of about fifty cut
in front of him and ordered loudly to the bar girl:

"A special coffee, Pamela!"

"Sindona Special!" somebody sitting at a table called out.

"Or a Pisciotta Special, which is the same thing," said
someone else.

Everyone laughed except for the inspector and Pamela.

For Pamela, it was probably because she hadn't understood the reference. For Montalbano, it was because the quips sent his cojones into a spin.

The poisoning of Michele Sindona, a banker, with a spiked coffee in his jail cell—exactly as had happened a few years earlier to Gaspare Pisciotta, the right-hand man of the infamous bandit Salvatore Giuliano—was the news of the day. By this expedient, the Italian-American banker, who was connected as much to the Mafia as to half the politicians in Italy, had been silenced forever.

Had he talked, and revealed all the collusion between the banks, the Mafia, and the political system, it would have been worse than a maximum-force earthquake. And so they'd resorted to a not-quite-legal expedient for maintaining state secrets. And truth and justice be damned.

"What'll it be?" Pamela asked Montalbano lazily, while buffing the bar with a rag.

She was a Milanese girl of twenty-five who had been working at the bar for about six months, a washed-out, slightly goatlike blonde, generally nondescript, with expressionless blue eyes like a doll's, clearly an airhead but, to make up for it, one endowed with a considerable bust and a pair of generous, bouncy buttocks.

When the inspector asked for an entire bottle of whisky, she remained speechless, opening her mouth wide in surprise, as if he'd asked for half the moon. She glanced at the shelf behind her, then at the inspector, and then again at the shelf. In the end she said:

"I've only got a quarter bottle left of this whisky. It's better if you ask at the cash register."

The cashier looked at his watch and grimaced.

"Inspector, we're about to close. It's almost midnight, and I've got nobody to send to the warehouse. I'm sorry."

"Then give me the quarter bottle."

The calculations over the value of that quarter bottle became a little prickly. The cashier suggested they calculate by the number of shots, whereas the inspector said it should cost a quarter of the price of a whole bottle. When they finally reached an agreement, Montalbano paid up and went home, finding that his desire for whisky had completely vanished. He left the bottle on the table, smoked a cigarette while looking at the sea, then went to bed.

The next morning at the office went by in dead calm. He started signing papers, which were backed up so high it was frightening. At one o'clock he went out to eat at Calogero's, then took a long walk along the jetty. He thought that if things continued this way, with nothing for him to do, it might be best for him to take a few days' leave and go see Livia in Boccadasse. When he got back to the station, he chatted with Augello and Fazio about Sindona's death. It seemed good ol' Italy was destined never to change its fine, time-tested customs, no matter what government was in charge.

It was already five o'clock when the internal phone rang. It was Catarella.

"Chief, 'ere'd be a soitain Signor Valletta onna premisses wantin' a talk t'yiz poissonally in poisson."

He didn't know any Valletta, but with Catarella you could never be sure about people's surnames.

"Send him in. You guys can stay, if you want."

Augello said he had something to do; Fazio remained.

Valletta's real name was, naturally, Barletta, Totò Barletta; he was the guy who had recently taken over the Caffè Castiglione.

"I'm worried an' I don' know what to do."

"What are you worried about?"

"Pamela, my bar girl, who normally comes in to work at two p.m., didn't show up today."

To the inspector this didn't seem like such a big deal. What could have happened to a girl so anonymous she barely seemed to exist?

"Signor Barletta, the girl's a legal adult, and to be honest, I don't think being three hours late—"

"But you have no idea how punctual an' meticulous that girl is! She's never a minute off! An' if she ever happens to be a little late, she calls in to let us know. Nah, Inspector, ya gotta believe me. There's somethin' not right about this."

"Have you tried calling her yourself?"

"Of course. The phone just rings and rings."

"Have you sent anyone over to Pamela's house?"

"I went there myself! I knocked, I called out, but nobody answered."

The girl was in good health, as the inspector had seen for himself the night before. But he asked anyway.

"Does she have any kind of illness?"

"She's healthy as an ox."

"Does she have any women friends?"

"I don't know any."

"Do you know if she has a boyfriend, or someone who—"

"No boyfriend, but all the men you could ask for. Single, married, young, old . . . She ain't picky, she likes 'em all."

"Care to explain a little better?"

"She changes men every coupla weeks at the most. Actually on average it lasts about a week. But it's not for money. That's just the way she is. You realize that, at this point, I should be asking half the people in town about Pamela. An' my questions could make a few guys uncomfortable, if they've got a little family. Know what I mean?"

Montalbano was sitting there, completely flabbergasted.

What? That washed-out, ditzy, characterless blonde, who always seemed half-asleep, was some kind of legendary man-eater? He had trouble believing it.

"Did you have some kind of argument with her?"

"Me? Why do you ask?"

"Well, as her work provider . . ."

"No, no, we never had any arguments."

"Do you have any possible explanation for her absence?"

"If I did, I woulda told you right away."

Montalbano decided to put an end to this.

"Listen, for now it would be a bit premature, to say the least, to start looking for her. I'll make you a deal. If by midnight tonight there's still no sign of the girl, you can come back here tomorrow morning, and we'll decide what to do."

Barletta seemed less than convinced as he left.

"You know anything about this girl?" Montalbano asked Fazio.

"The same things Barletta told you."

"Can you explain to me what these guys see in her?"

"Apparently in bed she's like some kind of inflatable doll, except that she's alive. She never says no to anything. But then she gets bored fast. And when she tells some guy she's had enough, that's it. There's no talking her out of it."

"Is it true she doesn't do it for money?"

"Chief, let's get one thing straight. She doesn't accept anything in cash, that's true. She says she does it for her own pleasure. But give her a present, and she won't turn it down. On the contrary. They say she's got two safety-deposit boxes at the Banca dell'Isola. The girl's found a gold mine in Vigàta!"

"But this manner of dumping one guy and picking up the next, hasn't it ever created tussles between any of the men frequenting her?"

"There's been a couple of incidents. The guys who got thrown out after she had no more use for them certainly weren't happy about it. But there's never been anything serious. Or, if there has, I haven't heard about it."

"What do *you* think could have happened?"

"Maybe she just ran off on some amorous fling and will be back in a couple of days. Or maybe she found someone she really flipped over. It sometimes happens to women like that."

———

As soon as he came into the station, just past eight o'clock, Catarella informed him that Signor Valletta had been waiting for him for the past half hour.

"Is Fazio in?"

"Yessir, onna premisses 'at'd be 'ese 'ere premisses, 'a'ss where 'e is."

"Tell him to come to my office, and then show Barletta in, too."

The two came in at the same time. Barletta looked worried and was holding some papers in his hand.

"Still no word of her," he said disconsolately.

"Would you like to file a missing persons' report?"

"Absolutely. I brought the papers."

"What papers?"

"Her contract with me, and a photocopy of her ID card . . . Pamela's real name wasn't Pamela, but Ernesta."

"All right, then, go with Signor Fazio into his office to draft the report, then the two of you come back here, and we'll all go to Pamela's house—er, Ernesta's, or whatever her name is."

After her husband died, Signora Rosalia Insalaco, a sixtyish woman as tubby as a barrel and covered with more necklaces and bracelets than the Madonna of Pompeii, had to make do with a measly pension, and so she got the brilliant idea to split her little suburban house into two apartments and rent out half of it.

This second apartment had a separate entrance at the rear of the house.

"Pamela wanted me to keep the extra key myself. But I'm no busybody, I want you to know."

Montalbano would have bet his family jewels that the minute Pamela was out of the house, the widow would always go and search her apartment, not sparing even the young woman's underwear.

"But, in spite of your discretion, you couldn't help but hear when Pamela was at home, correct?"

"Inspector, what can I say? Even if I didn't want to, I could actually hear her breathing."

"How long has it been since she came home?"

"Two nights. Of that I'm absolutely sure. It's been total silence, not a sound."

"All right, now give me the key. I'll come back to you afterwards."

Barletta stood up to follow him.

"No, sir. You stay here and keep the lady company."

A tiny entrance with a small arch framing a long hallway with five doors, three on the left and two on the right. Kitchen, bathroom, large closet, bedroom, sitting room. Everything very clean, floors shiny as mirrors, dishes in the kitchen looking as if they'd never been used.

The most interesting things were found in the bedroom, where, in addition to a spacious double bed with a nightstand on either side and a television with a videocam, but no cassettes, there was a large armoire. Pamela possessed an incredible quantity of bras and panties, all expensive, provocative stuff, predominantly black in color.

But the real find was in one of the four drawers of the armoire.

It was shut with a little lock that Fazio had no trouble opening, and contained eight agendas, the most recent for the present year.

In them Pamela would write down, with the care of an accountant or bookkeeper, the name of the lover on duty for that week or fortnight. And on the day of their first meeting, she also wrote down the person's telephone number.

And she noted the presents she received. A bracelet here, a pair of earrings there, a necklace . . .

"You gonna want to look at all these diaries?" Fazio asked.

The inspector wasn't interested in the girl's amatory past.

"Nah, I'll just take the current one. Pamela's only been in Vigàta for six months."

"I don't think there's much else to see in here."

They returned to the other side of the house.

2

"Find anything?" Barletta asked anxiously as soon as they reappeared.

"Not a thing," replied Montalbano, who didn't see why he should have to report everything to him.

But he caught sight of the expression of surprise on the widow's face. She must certainly have known of the existence of the diaries in the armoire. And he would have bet she'd opened the lock and thumbed through all of them, page after page.

"Signora Insalaco, does Pamela have a cleaning woman?"

"Yessir, she does. I found her one myself. A dependable woman. Her name's Agata Gioeli. She's also got a copy of the house key. She comes every morning from eleven to two. She also cooks for her, and when Pamela gets up, usually around noon, she tidies up the bedroom. It was Agata who came and told me that Pamela hadn't come back the night before, because the bed was still made."

"Was this the first time that's happened?"

"Yes."

"And how did she usually find the bed?" Montalbano asked mischievously.

"We can talk about it, if you like," the widow said with some reservation and a twisted grin.

"Some other time. So Agata should be here soon?"

"Yessir."

"Tell her please to come to the police station. Does Pamela have a car?"

Barletta answered.

"What's she need a car for? It's a fifteen-minute walk from here to the café."

"Anyway, almost every night she had someone to drive her home," added the widow.

"So you would hear them arrive and then leave?"

"Of course. But it's not like they left right away."

"How much later, normally?"

"It depended. One hour, two hours, three hours, even four . . ."

So the widow would stay up listening to everything Pamela did.

"I see. We'll talk about that again later, if need be. For now I have to say good-bye. I thank you for your cooperation."

"And what should I do?" Barletta asked as they were leaving.

"I'll let you know if there are any new developments," said Montalbano, to cut things short.

A perusal of Pamela's agenda revealed that the lover scheduled for that Sunday night, one Carlo Puma, was to see his term expire after that night, and the torch was to have been picked up on Monday night and carried forward by a certain Enrico De Caro. Pamela had written down both of their phone numbers.

The inspector decided to let a little time pass before bothering them. It was better to tiptoe around this thing for the moment. Otherwise, if the girl reappeared in a few days, as was likely, he would have raised a big cloud of dust for nothing.

Agata, the cleaning lady, was a tall, slender woman of about fifty with sharp eyes and a quick tongue. Montalbano wanted Fazio to be present for the meeting.

"As far as we've been able to gather, Miss Pamela didn't like to sleep alone at night," the inspector began diplomatically.

Agata threw her head back and emitted a long laugh that sounded rather like a horse's whinny.

"Sleep at night? Are you kidding? That girl didn't sleep at night—she usually fell asleep around dawn!"

"How can you say that? You weren't there."

"Oh, that would've been all I needed, to be there! But when the young lady finally did make up her mind to get up and I went into the bedroom, it was like stepping onto a battlefield! For instance, sometimes they would do it right on the box spring, throwing the mattresses onto the floor; other times they would move the bed so they could see their reflection in the mirror on the armoire; other times they would move the armoire; then on other nights they'd do the TV thing . . ."

"What TV thing?" Montalbano and Fazio asked in unison.

They were thinking the same thing: *Want to bet that Pamela liked to videotape her athletic feats?*

"They'd watch on TV these films of men and women screwing their eyeballs out."

Fazio exchanged a quick glance with Montalbano.

"How come we didn't find any films like that?" Fazio asked her.

"Because about ten days ago the young lady sold them to a man who paid her well for them," replied Agata. "I was there."

"Do you know who he was?"

"Yessir, his name's Giuseppe Cosentino."

"Do you know this man's phone number or address?"

"No, sir."

Montalbano thumbed through Pamela's diary and had a stroke of luck. He found Cosentino's name and phone number. Beside it was the word: *cassettes*.

But the housekeeper hadn't finished telling the story of the state she would find the house in when she came in the morning.

"But it wasn't just the bedroom! Nosirree! They had to do it in the bathtub, too! With the shower running, flooding the whole goddamn place! Or on the two armchairs in the living room! An' sometimes, I'm not kidding, on the kitchen table! Right when they were eating something, they'd get the urge and throw the tablecloth on the floor with everything on it! And—"

"Listen," Montalbano said, interrupting her, "did the young lady ever mention to you any quarrels she may have had with her nightly companions?"

"What, you think she's gonna tell me about something like that? I was just the cleaning lady. She never confided in me."

"Did the young lady ever receive any phone calls when you were in the house?"

"Now and then."

"Were you able to hear whether—"

Agata Gioeli gave her horsey laugh.

"Mr. Inspector, the phone would ring and ring, but she never answered and didn't want me to, either."

"Why wouldn't she answer?"

"Because she was a walking corpse! She would shuffle around the house with her hands out in front of her, like a sleep-walker! All dazed from lack of sleep and too much fucking! She could only start talking after she'd had at least five coffees!"

"Do you have any idea why she might have disappeared?"

"Nah. I only know one thing, that if the young lady don't come back, I'm gonna lose a month's pay."

After Agata left, Fazio made a philosophical observation.

"So, we're looking at a girl who, even with all the affairs she had, seems not to have any history."

"You're exactly right. In fact, we don't even know whether she ran away of her own volition or was disappeared. So let's start trying to give some substance to all these words."

He consulted the diary again, turned on the speaker-phone, and dialed a number.

"Hello?"

"Is this Giuseppe Cosentino?"

"Yes, it is. Who's calling?"

"This is Inspector Montalbano, police."

"Ah."

A pause.

"Can't you talk?"

"I'm in a meeting."

"Any idea why I'm calling?"

"Yes. But, I'm terribly sorry, but at the moment I can't . . .
His Excellency the bishop is here and—"

"Just one question. Was it you who bought some certain
videocassettes from a young woman you know?"

"Yes."

"Thank you."

He hung up.

"So this tallies with what Agata told us. As you can see,
we have to tread on some slippery, maybe dangerous turf. It's
possible that among those sharing Pamela's wild nights there
may be some high rollers. So we need to—"

The internal phone rang, interrupting him.

"Chief, 'ere'd a happen a be a Signor Fuma onna premisses 'oo wants a talk t'yiz poissonally in poisson."

"Wait a second."

He turned to Fazio.

"You know anyone named Fuma?"

"No, I don't think so."

"Ask him what he wants to talk to me about," he said to
Catarella.

A few minutes went by. Then Catarella returned.

"'E don't wanna tell me, Chief. 'E says 'e'll tell yiz over
the phone if I go away."

"Okay."

A moment later a stifled male voice said:

"This is Carlo Puma. I want to talk to you about Pamela."

"Come in at once."

Then, turning to Fazio, the inspector said:

"It's Carlo Puma, Pamela's last lover."

He was a man in his mid-forties with a distinguished air and good manners. But he was clearly nervous and upset.

"Please sit down. What have you got to tell me?"

"I'd rather speak to you alone."

"I'm sorry, Signor Puma, but my colleague Fazio stays. If you don't like it, you can leave."

Puma remained seated and wiped the sweat from his brow with a handkerchief.

"It's not easy for me . . . I came of my own accord to prevent any vicious rumors from . . . I'm a town councilor, president of the business consortium, and I wouldn't want . . ."

"Mind if I help you out a little?" Montalbano asked.

"How?"

"By telling you, for example, that you were going to spend Sunday night with Pamela, and that was to be your last night after the six previous ones."

Puma very nearly fell out of his chair. He just sat there, mouth agape, trying to catch his breath.

"But . . . how . . . how do you know that?"

Montalbano showed him the daybook.

"Pamela wrote down the names and phone numbers of all her lovers."

"Oh, my God!" Puma wailed.

"Tell me about Sunday night," said Montalbano.

Making a visible effort, Puma managed to calm down a little.

"I'd arranged with Pamela, ever since the first time, that I would wait for her in my car, in Vicolo Caruana, at around a quarter past midnight. When she walked by, I would get out of the car and follow her on foot."

"Why not park outside the front door and wait for her there?"

"Because Pamela told me her landlady was a very nosy busybody and often took down the license plate number of the people who drove her home."

"I see. Go on."

"On Sunday I was at Vicolo Caruana at midnight. I had a little present for her."

"What was it?"

"A bracelet . . . a rather expensive one. I waited until one o'clock, and I began to get worried, because she's usually so punctual . . . So I started up the car and drove past her house, but there were no lights on inside. I got out and rang the bell, but nobody answered. So I went to the café, but it was closed. And that's the whole story. The following evening I heard she'd disappeared."

"Did Pamela ever talk to you about having problems with any of her ex-lovers?"

Puma became uncomfortable.

"We never really talked much . . . You see, I could only stay at her place for as long as necessary, after which I had to get home by a certain hour, otherwise my wife . . ."

"I see. If you have anything else to tell us—"

"If it's possible to keep my name—"

"I'll try to leave you out of it."

After Puma left, Fazio took a negative view of things.

"He didn't tell us anything new."

"But he did imply something that raises a question. How many streets are there that link the café to Pamela's house? Puma didn't see her on Vicolo Caruana, but is that the only street she could have taken? Isn't it possible Pamela didn't feel like seeing him and took another route? And isn't it also possible that Pamela never got as far as Vicolo Caruana?"

"What do you say we go for a little walk?" Fazio suggested.

Montalbano agreed.

3

Before they left the station, Fazio rang Barletta and asked him to carefully explain the route that Pamela usually took to go home from work.

Then they went out and followed this route step by step, according to the directions they'd been given. They calculated that on average it took about twenty minutes to cover the distance.

Pamela could also get to her house by way of another small street, though this one had been blocked at one end to cars as well as pedestrians, due to ongoing work on the sewers.

Ergo: That night, Pamela, after leaving the café, definitely walked some twenty yards along the Corso, turned right, probably took Salita Gomez uphill, after which she crossed Viale della Vittoria and took Via Indipendenza, but she quite certainly never turned right again onto Vicolo Caruana.

Montalbano suggested they go to the café and get further clarifications from Barletta.

"Last Sunday, when you were closing, who were the last people to leave the establishment?"

"I dunno, 'cause I wasn't here. You can ask the cashier," said Barletta, falling in behind them.

The cashier didn't hesitate for a second.

"As usual, the last people out were Pamela, Pitrino the waiter, and me. I'm the one who lowers and raises the shutters."

"Was there anyone outside waiting for Pamela?"

"Out here in front, no, sir. But you should ask Pitrino. He walked with her for a ways that evening."

Pitrino, the waiter, a skinny man of sixty with eyeglasses like the bottoms of Coke bottles, declared that since he lived halfway up Salita Gomez, he'd walked that way with the girl. It wasn't the first time they'd done that, though often Pamela had someone waiting for her in their car and didn't need to be accompanied. No, nobody had stopped her along the way.

At this point the inspector asked Pitrino a routine question.

"What kind of mood was Pamela in?"

The response took them all by surprise.

"She wasn't the same as usual. Actually, to tell you the truth, I'd never seen her so nervous. She kept turning around to look behind her, like she was afraid someone might be coming after her. When somebody walked past her she grabbed my arm, and I could feel her trembling . . ."

Montalbano hurried back to the cashier.

"Please try and answer my questions as precisely as possible. Did anything happen that afternoon or evening that could have upset Pamela?"

"No, there wasn't anything like that."

"An argument with a customer, a rude comment . . ."

"No, nothing at all."

"Think it over carefully, because the waiter says that when Pamela left here, she was very agitated."

"Ah!" said the cashier. "Maybe it was the phone call."

"She got a phone call?"

"Our phone's right here—see?—at the cash register. So I'm always the one who picks up. The customers were already all gone when it rang. Some man said he wanted to talk to Pamela. Me and Pitrino went out to pull down the first two shutters. She was just setting down the receiver when I came back in."

"So it was a long phone call?"

"Yeah."

"If we assume that she was in fact kidnapped, the kidnapper can only be someone who knew what route Pamela took to walk home. And I'm convinced that the kidnapping occurred when she was about to cross Viale della Vittoria, which is broad and cars can drive pretty fast on it," said Montalbano.

"But the question isn't where, it's why," said Fazio. "And maybe the explanation for everything is in that phone call."

"If we could somehow find a motive, it would be a big help," the inspector admitted.

They sat there for a few moments, thinking. Then Montalbano had an idea.

"Take Pamela's daybook and write down all the names and numbers you can find in it. Try and see if there's anyone with the Mafia or who's had any trouble with the law."

"And what if I find something?"

"If you find something, then tell me."

"And after I tell you, then what?"

"Are you trying to bust my chops, Fazio? When we're wandering in the dark like we're doing, even the light from a match is better than nothing. And while we're at it, let's keep going. Turn on the speakerphone and get me Barletta on the line."

"Signor Barletta? Montalbano here. Since you've already filed a missing persons' report, why don't you see if you can get a little help from TeleVigàta or the Free Channel and send them the photo of Pamela that's on her ID card? Sound like a good idea? Yes? Then get on it right away, so it'll be broadcast on tonight's news."

He ended the call and turned to Fazio.

"The last name in her diary is Enrico De Caro, the lover who never got his turn. Give him a call and ask him to come in here tomorrow morning at nine."

When he walked into the station the next morning, Fazio told him that De Caro was very sorry but had an engagement that morning that he couldn't postpone, so he would come that afternoon.

Fazio hadn't finished speaking when the phone rang.

"Chief, 'ere's a Signor Pirtuso onna line 'at wants a talk t'yiz—"

"Poissonally in poisson?"

"Yessir. Howdja guess?"

"Never mind. But I don't know any Pirtuso."

"How can ya say ya don' know 'im, Chief? 'E's the prizidint o' the Sicilian Bank!"

"But then his name is Verruso, not Pirtuso!"

"Why, wha'd I say? Pirtuso."

"Put him on," said the inspector, turning on the speaker-phone. "Good morning, sir, what can I do for you?"

"I urgently need to talk to you, but unfortunately I can't come to your office."

"Talk to me about what?"

"About the girl who disappeared, the bar girl from the Castiglione."

"We'll be right over."

Bank President Verruso, bowing ceremoniously, showed them into his office and closed the door.

"I'll get straight to the point," he began. "Last night, on the midnight news report on TeleVigàta, I learned that Ernesta Bianchi, who goes by the name of Pamela, had disappeared. She's . . . a client of ours. Have there been any new developments since then?"

"None."

"If I've understood correctly, she disappeared sometime Sunday night, is that right?"

"That's right," said Montalbano.

"But that's not possible," said the banker.

"Why not?"

"Because at eight o'clock Monday morning, which is when we open, the young lady was here, at the bank."

Montalbano's and Fazio's eyes opened wide.

"To do what?" asked the inspector.

"As I said, she's a client of ours. She has a checking account and two safety-deposit boxes with us."

"Did she make a withdrawal?"

"Yes, but only in the sense that she withdrew everything

and closed the account. She also took what was in the two safety-deposit boxes. She had a medium-sized suitcase with her and put everything in it."

"Can you tell me how much was in her account?"

"I'm sorry, but I can't. All I can say is that Barletta paid her well, she earned a lot in tips, and she was a great economizer."

"Did she tell you why she was closing the account and the deposit boxes?"

"She alluded vaguely to a sudden death that forced her to return to Milan. But . . ."

"But?" Montalbano encouraged him.

"I wouldn't want . . . it's just an impression of mine . . . without . . . Well, she seemed to me very, very afraid."

"It's starting to seem clear that we're looking at a voluntary disappearance," Fazio said as they were heading back to the station.

"More than a disappearance, it was a sudden, precipitous flight," Montalbano countered. "And what's clear is that what brought it on was that telephone call she got as the café was closing. Apparently the man on the phone threatened her so severely that Pamela decided to run away as soon as possible."

"But where could she have spent the night?" asked Fazio.

"If we start asking questions, we'll never get to the end of it," said the inspector. "You said she was a girl with no history? Well, you were dead wrong. She's got a history, all right, and a complicated one at that. The only problem is, we don't know how to read it."

Catarella assailed him in the entranceway.

"Ahh, Chief! A Signor Sconsolato called tree times oigently wantin' a talk t'yiz!"

"All right, when he calls back, put him through to me."

They'd barely sat down when the phone rang.

"Is this Inspector Montalbano?"

"Yes."

"I'm Mario Consolato."

"What can I do for you?"

"Listen, I wouldn't want there to be any misunderstandings. I'm a good person, a good father, an honest businessman, and I've never had any problems with the law!"

"I'm glad to hear."

"So I don' want anyone to think that if I knew this girl it was because . . . you know, I was doin' it with her."

"What girl are you talking about?"

"Pamela."

"Tell me everything."

"I don' live in Vigàta. I live in Montereale, but I come to Vigàta almost daily. And I heard on the TV news that this Pamela, the bar girl at the Castiglione, supposedly disappeared Sunday night. Is that right?"

"It appears to be."

"There, you said 'appears to be'—'cause, on Monday morning, around nine-thirty, I gave her a ride in my car."

"Tell me everything in the proper order."

"All right, I'll do just that. As I said, I live in Montereale. On Monday morning I had to go to Montelusa, and so I drove through Vigàta, and there, on the Corso, just past the Banca dell'Isola, around nine-thirty at the latest, I spotted Pamela with a suitcase in her hand, heading towards the taxi stand. And so I pulled over and asked her if she wanted a ride to Montelusa. She said okay and got in the car. When we got there, she had me drop her off at the station."

"Did she tell you at any time during the ride why she was leaving Vigàta?"

"Inspector, she never once opened her mouth. Except to thank me and say good-bye."

"Was she nervous or worried?"

"She was terrified, Inspector. So badly that I asked her what had happened to her, if someone had done something to her, but she wouldn't answer."

"What trains normally leave at around ten in the morning?" Fazio wondered aloud.

"Call and find out."

The answer was that there was a train for Palermo at ten-fifteen.

"She would've taken that train even if it was going to Istanbul," said the inspector. "The important thing was for her to get as far away as possible, as quickly as possible."

"But what could she have done that was so dangerous that it would lead to such a frightening telephone call?"

"Certainly something that had to do with her nighttime escapades. Speaking of which, did you draw up that list?"

"Not yet."

"Do it soon."

Fazio shrugged.

"What's the rush? At any rate, I don't think we're gonna hear any more about this girl."

"What makes you so sure? In the meantime, De Caro's going to come and talk to us this afternoon."

4

Enrico De Caro, who didn't show up until almost seven p.m., was a well-dressed man of about thirty, rather likable, alert, intelligent, and not the least bit upset at being summoned to the police department.

"Sorry I'm late, but I'm the political secretary for the—"

"No need to apologize. I thank you for coming. Do you know why I wanted to see you?"

"Inspector, the only possible reason could be that I was planning to spend a few nights with Pamela starting Monday. Is that right?"

"That's right."

"But tell me something. How did you find out?"

"Pamela wrote everything down in her diary, including first and last names and telephone numbers."

De Caro didn't seem especially worried.

"Really? How silly!"

"You probably have nothing to say to us, but I wanted to meet you anyway, because . . ."

De Caro started laughing, cutting off the inspector.

"But I have a great many things to tell you!"

"About Pamela?"

"Absolutely!"

"Then go ahead."

"Well, Inspector, Pamela had planned that I would go to her place starting Monday because she hadn't wanted to come to my place, as I'd suggested. I live alone, you see. I'm single."

"So what happened?"

"What happened was that Sunday evening, around midnight, she called to ask me if she could come immediately to my place and spend the night there. I was pleasantly surprised and said yes. When I asked her why she'd changed her mind, she said she couldn't stay on the phone and would explain it to me later."

"Did she tell you where she was calling from?"

"The Caffè Castiglione."

Fazio and Montalbano exchanged glances. The girl had clearly called De Caro right after getting the phone call that had scared her to death.

De Caro continued:

"When I opened the door, she was standing there pale as a corpse and very upset. Once inside, she started crying desperately. I'd never seen her that way. I didn't know what to do. So I made her some chamomile tea, and she finally calmed down a little."

"Did you ask her what had happened?"

"Of course. But she didn't give me a clear answer. There were long silences, and every so often she would say a few disjointed things in incomplete sentences, but always repeating that she didn't do it."

"Didn't do what?"

"Well, from what I could gather, she'd received a telephone call from a man, an ex-lover, who seriously threatened to kill her, saying her hours were numbered."

"Did she tell you his name?"

"No. But she did say that he was someone who would definitely be capable of killing her. She told me she didn't want to have anything to do with this man—he was physically repellent to her—but in the end she'd been forced to go with him because he'd had her assaulted by two young toughs who actually tore all her clothes off."

"But why was he threatening her?"

"Apparently the guy had received a letter from Pamela asking for ten million lire in exchange for her silence about their relationship. She seems to have had in her possession a very compromising note from this man. If he didn't pay up, she would ruin his life. Except that Pamela swore up and down to me that she knew nothing about this blackmail, and she seemed sincere to me."

"But couldn't she just call the guy and clear things up?"

"That's what I suggested, but she said it would be useless, because it seemed clear to her that the man was convinced it was her. So I told her she should do something to convince him, and send back to the man the compromising note he'd written to her. But she replied that she didn't have it anymore. She'd noticed sometime before. Maybe she'd thrown it away, she couldn't remember. So she came to the conclusion that the only thing to do was to leave Vigàta. I advised her to go to the police, but she wouldn't hear of it. She only wanted to run away. So I had her lie down for a few hours, but she never fell asleep. In the morning she went into the bathroom, and I made her coffee. Then she asked me if I had a suitcase she could use, and I gave her one. I have nothing more to tell you."

"So that completes the picture," said Montalbano. "But we'll never know who the man that threatened her was. Oh, well.

And I think you're right, Fazio: That's probably the last we'll hear of Pamela."

He was dead wrong.

A report on the Free Channel's eight-thirty evening news program hit Montalbano like a club to the head.

> *At around five p.m. this afternoon, during an inspection of the two tunnels along the line between Montelusa Alta and Montelusa Bassa, a railway technician discovered the body of a woman in the second tunnel, mistaking it at first for a pile of rags. Summoned at once to the scene, the police initially concluded that it had probably been an accident due to the inattention of the traveler, who they conjectured had accidentally opened the door and fallen out, crashing against the ballast and expiring at once. However, after a summary examination, the coroner, Dr. Pasquano, declared that the victim had been strangled before being thrown out of the train, and that the murder had occurred on Monday morning. The recovery of the victim's purse a few yards away from her body has allowed authorities to identify her as Ernesta Bianchi, born in Milan twenty-six years ago.*
>
> *The investigation into the murder has been assigned to Inspector Barresi, chief of the Montelusa Homicide Unit.*

He turned off the TV and rang Fazio. The line was busy.

The sense of agitation that had suddenly come over him wouldn't allow him to keep still. He walked around the table five times and tried Fazio's number again. It was free.

"Fazio, have you heard?"

"Yeah. I called a friend of mine with Montelusa Homicide to find out whether they also found the suitcase beside the body."

"Did they?"

"No."

"Come immediately to my place and bring her agenda. The killer's name is in there."

Fazio must have driven over a hundred miles an hour, because ten minutes later he was knocking at the door.

They sat down at the small dining room table. Montalbano started dictating all the names in the agenda, as Fazio wrote them down on a sheet of paper in front of him.

When they came to the name Michele Turrisi, who'd frequented Pamela four months after her arrival in Vigàta, Fazio made an exclamation of surprise.

"That's a name I wasn't expecting."

"Why?"

"Turrisi is a former hitman for the Sinagras who's made a career as the family accountant. He's married to Agostino Sinagra's niece."

"Let's keep going."

When they got to the end, they concluded that the person who stood the most to lose by being blackmailed by Pamela was indeed Michele Turrisi. The Sinagras would have made him pay dearly for his adulterous betrayal. And as poor Pamela had pointed out, he was someone who wouldn't think twice before killing someone.

"What are we gonna do?" asked Fazio.

"I'll tell you in a second," said Montalbano, who'd started getting dressed again.

"You want to go to Turrisi's house?"

"Are you kidding? Did you come here in a squad car?"

"Yeah. But what've you got in mind?"

"I think I get it now. I'm convinced it wasn't Pamela who sent that letter."

"Then who was it?"

"Do you remember the reason why Carlo Puma wouldn't park outside Pamela's front door?"

"No."

"Because Signora Rosalia Insalaco, the landlady, would sometimes take down the license plate number of the cars of Pamela's boyfriends."

"You're right!" said Fazio, slapping himself loudly on the forehead.

"Now, say the signora takes down a number at random and manages to find out that the car belongs to someone named Michele Turrisi, and so she decides to send him a nice little blackmail letter, pretending that it's Pamela who's writing it. The problem is that Signora Insalaco's an idiot and is making a huge mistake. She has no idea who she's dealing with."

"What do you intend to do?"

"I'm going to scare her out of her wits, so she knows how Pamela felt. But in a different way."

"What are you going to say to her?"

"I'll improvise, based on how she responds. Gimme her number."

He turned on the speakerphone, and as soon as the widow

picked up, Montalbano started talking in a breathless, panting voice.

"Signora Insalaco? Inspector Montalbano here."

"But I was just falling asleep!"

"For heaven's sake, don't! Try to remain as awake as possible! For your own good! Did you hear about Pamela on television?"

"I only use the TV to watch movies."

"So you didn't hear? Well, signora, listen to me very carefully. I want you to do exactly what I tell you. Your very life may depend on it. Got that? *Your life.*"

"My life? Oh, my God! What happened? Oh, dear God! Oh, my blessed little Jesus! But what happened?"

"Pamela was kidnapped by a mafioso, a cold-blooded killer, named Michele Turrisi, who mistakenly believed that the girl was trying to blackmail him. Pamela managed to convince him it wasn't true, so Turrisi let her go and she came to us. And she told us that Turrisi is now convinced that you wrote the letter of blackmail, Signora Insalaco, and he's on his way to your house now to kill you."

"*Oh, matre santa!* He's gonna kill me! Help! Help! Oh, Jesus, Mary, and Joseph, please save my soul! I'm gonna die!"

"No, signora, don't scream, don't cry, just listen to me. Don't open your door to anyone. Just pack a small suitcase with a few items and we'll be at your place in fifteen minutes. We'll take you somewhere safe."

"Oh, hurry, please! *Oh, matruzza santa*, help me!"

"Oh, and be sure to bring the note that Turrisi wrote to Pamela. And try to calm down. Don't worry, we'll get there in time to protect you. But I repeat: Don't open the door to anyone but me."

And he hung up.

"Now comes the second act of the comedy. We have to pull up at the signora's house at maximum speed with the sirens on full blast and come to a screeching halt. We'll get out of the car brandishing our revolvers, and as soon as she opens the door, you're going to grab her and put her in the car, while I get the suitcase and close the door."

"Where we gonna take her?"

"To the station."

The whole thing went a little differently, in that as soon as the widow opened the door and saw the inspector, she fainted from the stress. It took both of them to load her into the car. But even at the station she couldn't stop crying desperately. Montalbano threw fuel on the fire by telling her about all of Turrisi's wicked deeds, making them up as he went along, stuff straight out of a horror film.

In the end, Rosalia Insalaco confessed that it was she who had written the letter.

And she gave Montalbano the note that she'd found among Pamela's papers and stolen.

It said:

> *To Pamela,*
>
> *In memory of the loving nights we spent together, I give you this necklace.*
>
> *Michele Turrisi*

The inspector put it in his pocket and said to Fazio:

"Please take the signora into your office. I have to make a phone call."

He dialed a number at Montelusa Central Police.

"Barresi? Montalbano here. Listen, if you could come over to my office, I'll tell you who killed Ernesta Bianchi and why. It was a double mistake. No, I'm not joking. And try to hurry, 'cause I'm a little tired."

1

Montalbano was fed up. He couldn't take it any longer. After glancing at his watch—it was almost twenty past five in the afternoon—he looked at Augello and Fazio, who were sitting in front of his desk, also feeling fed up.

"Boys," he said, "we've been talking about this question of night shifts for over two hours without arriving at any solution. But I have a great idea I want to propose."

He never had a chance to propose his great idea, however, because a bomb, surely thrown in through the open window, went off in the room, deafening them all.

Or, more precisely, such was the terrible impression all three of them had. At any rate, Fazio fell out of his chair, Augello threw himself forward onto the floor, shielding his head with his hands, and the inspector found himself kneeling behind his desk.

"Anyone hurt?" Montalbano asked a moment later.

"Not me," said Augello.

"Me neither," said Fazio.

They fell silent.

Because, as they were saying this, they all realized that it wasn't a bomb that had made that frightening boom, but the door to Montalbano's office, which, flung open, had crashed against the wall.

And, indeed, in the doorway stood Catarella, who this time did not, however, "papologize" or "beck their parting," but merely excused himself, saying his hand had slipped.

He was red in the face and trembling all over, his eyes so goggled they looked like they were about to pop out of his head.

"Th-th-they-sh-sh-shat-th-th-the-po-po-pope!" he said in a voice that came out very shrill, like one of the Flying Squad's sirens.

And he started weeping uncontrollably.

None of the three, ears still ringing from the boom, understood a thing. But clearly something terrible had happened.

Montalbano went up to him, put his arm on his shoulder, and spoke paternally to him.

"Come on, Cat, get ahold of yourself."

Meanwhile Fazio brought a glass of water, and Montalbano made Catarella drink it. It seemed to calm him down.

"Sit down," Fazio said to him, indicating his chair.

Catarella shook his head in refusal. He would never sit in Montalbano's presence.

"Speak slowly and tell us what happened," said Augello.

"They shot the pope," said Catarella.

He said it quite clearly. It was the others who didn't understand or couldn't believe what they'd heard.

"What did you say?!" asked Montalbano.

"They shot the pope," Catarella repeated.

The others remained spellbound for a few seconds. The pope couldn't possibly have been shot. It was inconceivable, and their brains, in fact, were refusing to accept the news.

"But where did you hear it?" the inspector asked.

"Onna radio."

Without saying a word, all three raced into Augello's office, where there was a television set. Augello turned it on. A reporter was saying that John Paul II, while standing up in his automobile, greeting the faithful in St. Peter's Square, had been struck by two shots from a revolver, one in the left hand and the other in his intestine. The latter injury was very serious. The pope had been taken to the Gemelli hospital. The gunman had tried to escape but was stopped by the crowd. He was a Turk of twenty-three by the name of Mehmet Ali Agca and belonged to a dangerous nationalist group called the Grey Wolves.

They remained glued to the TV set until half past seven, hoping to find out more. But they didn't learn anything else, other than the fact that the pope was teetering between life and death.

"Do you understand any of this?" Fazio asked Montalbano.

"Not a thing. But it's starting to look like a bad year. Between the Mafia, the P2, the Sindona case, the negotiations with the Camorra in Naples over the liberation of Ciro Cirillo, and now this Turk shooting the pope . . ."

"Maybe it's the KGB getting even for all the chaos in Poland," Augello ventured.

"Anything's possible," said Montalbano.

━━━

Driving through town on his way to Marinella, he noticed that there were very few people on the streets, no doubt all at home in front of their television sets. When he got home, he realized he wasn't hungry.

Montalbano was not a man of the church. In fact, he considered himself an agnostic and generally didn't like priests. Still, this whole affair seemed rather ugly and upset him. And, truth be told, he felt scared. Because he was unable to understand what kind of motives anyone could have for wanting to assassinate the pope.

Was somebody trying to trigger a religious war? Was it the act of a lone madman? Or was it an international plot, the aims and possible consequences of which remained unknown?

He went and looked for a portable radio, small but powerful, which he'd bought a year earlier. It picked up stuff from all over the world. Taking it out onto the veranda, he turned it on. There wasn't a single station that wasn't talking about the attack, and even if the report was in Ostrogothic, at a certain point he would hear the word "pope" or the pope's name. But there was no news on the Vatican Radio. They were praying.

He spent some two hours in this fashion. Then he got up, went into the kitchen, made himself a salami sandwich, and went back out onto the veranda to eat it.

He kept listening to the radio until Livia called him just before midnight.

"Have you heard the awful news?"

"Of course."

"What do you think?"

"No idea."

"Listen, I wanted to confirm that I'll be arriving on the four o'clock flight tomorrow."

"I'll come and pick you up at the airport."

"No, why bother? There's a perfectly decent bus service.

But if you want, you can come and pick me up in Montelusa. The bus gets in at six-thirty."

"Okay, I'll be there."

They talked a little while longer, exchanged kisses over the phone, and wished each other good night. When he got into bed, Montalbano set the alarm for six.

The first thing he did when he woke up was to turn on the radio, and he learned that the operation on the pope had gone well. Feeling relieved, he went and opened the French door to the veranda. The day promised to be friendly, the sea was smooth as a mirror, and there wasn't a cloud in the sky. He went into the kitchen and made coffee, drank down a mugful, smoked a cigarette on the veranda, then shut himself in the bathroom.

When he came back out, he was surprised to find Adelina standing in front of him.

"Why so early?"

"Since I wenna the early Mass to pray f'the pope, I decided a come anna givva the house a nice-a goo' cleanup."

"Good idea, because Livia's coming this evening to stay for a few days."

"Ah . . ." said Adelina.

She turned her back to him and went into the kitchen. Montalbano stood there, speechless. Clearly she was not pleased that Livia was coming. But why? What had happened between the two women? He decided that the matter should be cleared up at once. But when he went into the kitchen, Adelina didn't give him any time to open his mouth.

"Isspector, I'm a-sorry, bu' less-a spick-a clearly. I'm a-no' gonna come 'ere onna days whenna young-a lady's 'ere."

"But why not?"

"'Cause iss-a betta tha' way."

"But did something happen?"

"Nuttin' an' everytin'."

"Care to explain?"

"Wha'ss t'asplain? We jess donna get along. She never like-a nuttin' I do. Iss never good enow. First issa bedsheet 'a'ss no' tight enow, 'enn issa bat'robe a'ss no' inna righ' place, 'enn iss a li'l bitta dust behine a TV . . . An' fuhgettabou' my cookin'! 'Ere's always too mucha salt, too li'l oil, anna so on . . . An' she herself donno even how ta cook a egg!"

On this last point, she was right.

"All right, now that you've got that off your chest . . ." Montalbano began.

"Now I gettit offa my chest iss no' gonna change-a nuttin'," Adelina said, interrupting him. "Iffa you like, I canna senn my cousin 'Gnazia for as long as a young-a lady's'ere."

"Does she cook as well as you?"

"Isspector, nobody cooka like-a me!"

Montalbano thought it over for a moment.

"Let's do this. Send your cousin 'Gnazia just to clean the house."

"An' what about eatin'?"

"This morning you can make some cold dishes for us to eat in the evening. After all, Livia won't be staying for more than three days."

"An' what abou' lunch?"

"I'll take her out to a trattoria."

"Okay," said Adelina. "I can do that."

At that moment the telephone rang. Montalbano went and picked up.

"Beckin' yer partin' f'callin' so oily inna mornin'," said Catarella.

"Something happen?"

"Wha' happen izzat 'ere was a boiglery."

"Did you inform Augello and Fazio?"

"Yessir, 'ey're already onna scene."

"Well, then, in that case . . ."

"Nah, nah, Chief, ya don' wanna take it too easy. Insomuch as how that Fazio juss called sayin' as how i' 'd be better if you was onna scene, too."

What?! His two detectives couldn't handle a simple burglary on their own? Montalbano huffed, but he couldn't very well back down.

"What's the address?"

"Via del Corso, stree' nummer toity-eight."

He ran into Adelina in the hallway. She was on her way out.

"Where are you going?"

"If I gotta cooka fuh tree days I's best a-go shoppin'."

"I'll give you a lift."

In the car, Adelina started talking about Livia again.

"Isspector, sir, you gotta 'scuse me for talkin' like I do, but I din't wanna talk about it wit' the young lady, so . . ."

"Don't worry about it, Adelí. The less we talk about it, the better."

———

Driving down the Corso, he realized something he hadn't noticed before. Which was that a grocery store and a wine shop had disappeared and been replaced by two banks. Was there really so much money in town that they needed to open two new bank branches?

Then, as if it had been scripted, number 38, Via del Corso, corresponded to one of the banks that hadn't been there before. A fancy sign, with neon tubes that lit up at night, announced that this was the Farmers' Bank of Montelusa.

He got out of the car. The rolling shutter was pulled almost down to the ground and showed no signs of having been forced. He tried to raise it, made an extra effort, but wasn't able. He rang the doorbell, which was on the wall under a plaque that also bore the bank's name.

Moments later a man's voice asked:

"Who is it?"

"Inspector Montalbano, police."

"I'll come and open up."

In a flash the shutter rose halfway. It must have functioned electrically. Montalbano bent down and passed under it.

In front of him he found a heavy armored door that worked by number combination, to be keyed in on a telephone-style touchpad. The door was open just enough to allow a person to enter.

They protected themselves well, at this bank.

There to receive him was an emaciated man of about fifty, all dressed in black and wearing a melancholy expression. He would have fit in better at a funeral home.

"Hello, I'm *ragioniere* Cascino. Downright shameful, don't you think?"

What was so shameful? The burglary? Did he have such

a lofty conception of banking that to be robbed was shameful? Why not just call it sacrilege?

Montalbano gave him a questioning look, and *ragioniere* Cascino felt pressed to explain.

"I was referring to the fact that the burglars showed no respect for the Holy Father, who just . . . Ah, never mind. Please, come in."

Montalbano went in.

2

Montalbano remembered that up until a couple of months ago the place had been a fancy barber shop called Today's Man. Outside there had been a display window with photos featuring a number of different male hairdos that had won prizes in hairstyling competitions. He'd never gone in, because at the time the sickly-sweet smell wafting out onto the sidewalk had sufficed to convince him there was no point.

The bank had tried to transform the interior into something a little less frivolous, but hadn't really succeeded, because the result now looked exactly like one of those government lottery offices of days past. Apparently this was some kind of third-tier bank.

Behind a wooden partition wall sat two cashiers at their stations. One of them, a young man, was watching a fly in the air, while the other, an elderly man, looked asleep. A third workstation, which must have belonged to the man who'd let him in, was vacant.

"Please follow me," *ragioniere* Cascino invited him in a tone of voice somewhere between that of a butler and an official guide.

Montalbano felt like he was visiting Windsor Castle.

The barber's large salon in the back had been turned into two smallish rooms. Over one of the doors was a little plaque with the word MANAGER. It was made of copper but was so bright it looked like solid gold. There was no sign on the other door, but to make up for this the door was made not of wood but some kind of heavy metal. And was more heavily armored than the entrance door. And it had, in fact, two combination dials with numbers on them.

Cascino knocked on the manager's door.

"Come in!" said a voice inside.

Ragioniere Cascino opened the door, poked his head inside, announced the arrival of the inspector, then ceremoniously withdrew.

"Please come in."

Damn, did they ever have a lot of frills and froufrous at this bank! It probably wasn't even this bad at the office of the president of the Bank of Italy!

Montalbano went in. Cascino closed the door behind him ever so quietly.

Fazio, who was sitting in front of the desk of a well-dressed fortyish man with a salon tan, stood up. The man did the same, adjusting his tie.

"Good morning," said Montalbano.

Was it just him, or could he still smell, ever so slightly, the sickly-sweet scent of the barbershop in the air?

"Where's Inspector Augello?" he asked Fazio.

"When he learned you were coming he left, saying he had some urgent business to attend to."

The little shit! He'd snuck off! The rotational spin of Montalbano's cojones, set in motion by the flap with Adelina, picked up considerable speed. Meanwhile, the tanned forty-year-old had come up to the inspector and held out his hand.

"My name is Vittorio Barracuda," he said. "I've heard so much about you, and I'm sorry to have to meet you in such unpleasant circumstances."

And he smiled, displaying two rows of teeth much like those of the dangerous carnivorous fish of the same name.

Montalbano was immediately convinced that the man before him would have a brilliant career in banking. A hungry wolf had more scruples than this guy. But wasn't he wasting his talent on a rinky-dink bank like this?

"How long has your bank been in Vigàta?"

"Six months."

"Have you established a good client base?"

"We can't complain."

"How many branches do you have in the province?"

"Just one. This one."

But didn't the bank call itself a "farmers' bank"? So why, then, hadn't they opened up branches in Cianciana or Canicattì, which were farming towns, instead of Vigàta, which was a fishing town?

Unable to stand Barracuda's toothy smile any longer, Montalbano turned to Fazio.

"Got anything to tell me?" he asked.

"The burglary occurred last night, Chief—"

"It would have been harder during the day," the inspector interrupted him gruffly.

Fazio realized the inspector was in a funk, pretended not to notice, and continued:

"—in the room next door, where the safety-deposit boxes are. If you want to go and have a look . . ."

"No, if anything we can do it later," Montalbano said curtly. "Can you tell me how many deposit boxes there are?"

"A hundred, but of varying sizes, of course."

"And were they all rented out?"

This time Barracuda answered.

"Yes, all of them."

Montalbano felt a little bewildered but didn't know why. There was something here that didn't add up, but he couldn't say what.

He'd remained standing ever since entering the room. He looked around. Barracuda intercepted his gaze.

"Please sit down," he said, freeing a chair by removing two binder files. Montalbano sat down.

"How did they get in?" he asked.

Fazio answered.

"They had the keys to the shutter and knew the combinations to the two armored doors, the one at the entrance and the one to the room with the deposit boxes."

"Wasn't there any kind of night guard?"

This time the manager answered.

"We use the services of the Securitas firm, which is very reliable."

"Did you give them a ring?" the inspector asked Fazio.

"Yeah, Chief. The watchman, whose name is Vincenzo

Larota, rides past every hour on his bike and didn't see any-thing."

"Apparently the burglars were aware of his schedule," the manager commented.

"Right," said the inspector.

But he said nothing else. He'd leaned forward and seemed engrossed in staring at the tips of his shoes.

To break the silence Barracuda tried to explain.

"You see, Inspector, we're a small bank, and so, together with management, we didn't think it necessary to resort to any kind of special surveillance . . ."

These words actually helped the inspector bring into focus the reason why he'd felt uneasy.

"What kind of customers do you have?" he asked.

Barracuda shrugged.

"We call ourselves a farmers' bank because our goal, so to speak, is indeed to help wine producers, citrus farmers, and the like, and to lend support to small farmers and local agri-cultural concerns . . ."

But where were all these agricultural concerns in the province of Montelusa? At any rate, in Vigàta you'd never find a single one even if you paid for their advertising.

"Naturally," Barracuda continued, "this branch is also seeking clients among the owners of fishing boats and the fishermen themselves . . ." He made a sly face and then added: "If the chief inspector of Vigàta Police would also like to become a customer of ours . . ."

And he laughed. Alone.

Montalbano, meanwhile, was asking himself some ques-tions. If these clients were all, when you came right down to it, poor bastards having trouble making ends meet, what need was there for a bank like this to have safety-deposit boxes? And not ten, mind you, but a hundred! Of varying size! And they'd all been rented! No, the whole thing made no sense at all.

Montalbano decided to aim straight for the bull's-eye.

"Could you please provide me with a complete list of the people renting the safety-deposit boxes?"

Barracuda immediately became as stiff as another kind of fish: salted cod.

"I don't see what use that would be."

"I'll determine that myself."

"Let me clarify."

"Yes, please clarify."

"The deposit boxes were all—I repeat, all—robbed without distinction. No specific boxes were targeted. Therefore—"

"Therefore you'll provide me with that list just the same," the inspector said, hardening his face.

Barracuda now turned from salted cod into frozen stockfish.

"But that, as I'm sure you know, would go against the rules of client confidentiality . . ."

"Signor Barracuda, I am not asking you to tell me the contents of the deposit boxes, which at any rate you don't even know yourself; I am only asking you for the list of the clients' names."

"I know, but I'll have to request authorization from senior management, and I'm not sure they'll—"

"How many of you know the combinations?" the inspector interrupted him, irritated.

"We all do. The three cashiers and myself."

"Do you change them often?"

"Every three days."

"Who's in charge of it?"

"I am. And I give the new combinations to those involved. I'll be changing them again this evening."

He gave the inspector a doubtful look.

"You're not thinking it was one of my employees who gave the combinations . . ."

Montalbano looked at him without saying anything. The manager continued.

"You know, there are devices that can—"

The inspector stopped him by raising his hand.

"I'm fully aware of that. I've seen some movies myself. I would appreciate it if, once I walk out of here, you would draw up a list of the bank personnel with names and telephone numbers and give it to my colleague here. I don't think there's any confidentiality restrictions in that regard."

He then asked Fazio:

"Have you called Forensics?"

"Not yet."

"Do it. I'll see you back at the station."

He stood up, and Barracuda held out his hand. Montalbano shook it and, while still holding it, wrinkled his nose.

"Can you smell it, too?" he asked.

"Smell what?" asked Barracuda, confused.

"There used to be a barber's salon here. I guess the walls have remained imbued with the scent. It's pretty unpleasant."

He had the impression that the bank manager's hand had become a little sweaty.

151

Stepping outside, he noticed that the morning was keeping its promise to be sensitive to his less-than-happy mood. He decided to go for a walk to the bank into which his salary was regularly deposited. Macaluso, the manager, received him immediately.

"What can I do for you, Inspector?"

"I need some information. How many safety-deposit boxes do you have at this bank?"

"Thirty."

"Could you tell me, at least roughly, how many deposit boxes the other banks in Vigàta have?"

"May I ask you the reason for these questions?" asked Macaluso.

News of the bank robbery hadn't spread. And it was better that way.

"It's for a survey the commissioner's office requested."

It took Macaluso only five minutes. It turned out that only the Montelusa Farmers' Bank had such a disproportionate number of boxes.

The bank manager looked at Montalbano in surprise.

"How strange! What do they do with all those safety-deposit boxes?"

"No idea," said the inspector, face as innocent as that of a cherub just then descended from heaven.

When he left the bank he retraced his steps, got in his car, and went to the office.

During the drive, something occurred to him. So that, once he got there, he gave his father a ring.

"What a wonderful surprise, Salvo! You have no idea how pleased I am to hear from you!"

"Papa, would you mind if I invited you to meet me for lunch at one?"

"Would I mind? What are you saying?!"

"All right, then, I'll see you at Calogero's at one."

3

When he got to the trattoria, his father was already seated at a small table set for two, waiting for him and watching the television, which was saying that while the prognosis for the pope was still guarded, his life was no longer in danger.

Seeing him come in, his father shot to his feet and went up to him with open arms.

Montalbano instinctively warded him off, extending his hand instead. His father pretended not to notice and shook it, smiling.

They both ordered the same first course, spaghetti with clam sauce. They'd always had the same tastes. His father was clearly dying of curiosity to know the reason for the unexpected invitation, but didn't venture to ask any questions.

They sat there in silence for a few moments, without even looking at each other. Then Montalbano made up his mind to speak.

"How's business?"

His father, who had a small wine-producing business between Montelusa and Favara, looked at him with surprise.

The last thing he'd expected to hear from his son, with whom he had a difficult relationship, was a question like that.

He sighed deeply, looked Montalbano in the eye, and shrugged.

"Not so great?"

"Not good at all. It's too small. We can't keep up with the competition. I'd have to expand it to give it any chance to survive, but I haven't got the money."

"Can't you ask for a loan at the bank?"

"Do you think that's so easy? One of them offered me an interest rate to make your hair stand on end; another refused me because my business partner had once contested a bill . . ."

The spaghetti arrived, and they spoke no more. Montalbano's father knew that his son didn't like to converse while eating. When they were done, they ordered a second course of fried mullet.

"So you're sailing on rough seas," Montalbano resumed.

"Yes."

"And what can you do to set things right?"

"A friend of mine from the Catania area suggested I become partners with him. His business does very well. I would sell mine to my partner, and that way—"

"Did you also try asking for a loan at the Montelusa Farmers' Bank?" Montalbano asked in an apparently indifferent tone.

The firm answer came at once.

"I never even went near the place."

"Why not?"

"There've been nasty rumors."

"Such as?"

His father twisted up his mouth.

"They're sharks pretending to be bighearted folks. I'll cite one example, which should be enough. A guy I know, by the

name of Divella, had signed some paper without really under-
standing what it said, and at some point found himself unable to
pay the interest rates, because they'd gone straight through the
roof. They ended up taking everything of his, even his house."

"Common criminals, in other words."

"Worse. Bloodthirsty animals."

"Have you ever heard mention of a certain Barracuda?"

"Sure! He's now the manager of the Vigàta branch. He's
the kind of guy who's capable of stabbing you in the back just
to stay in shape."

He heaved another sigh and then continued.

"But now let's change the subject, or I'm gonna lose my
appetite. Let's talk about you. Working a lot?"

The inspector didn't feel the least bit like talking about
himself. He started saying the standard things when he was
luckily interrupted by the arrival of the mullet.

After they'd finished eating, at the moment of saying
good-bye his father said, with a bitter smile:

"Well, even if you invited me because you needed some
information, I've really enjoyed seeing you just the same."

Montalbano felt like a worm.

He got into his car, but instead of going to the office, he took
the road to Montelusa. Pulling up outside the provincial headquarters of the Guardia di Finanza, the Finance Police, he
went inside, identified himself, and asked to speak with Marshal Antoci, whom he'd first met during the course of an investigation, and they'd instantly hit it off.

He told him about the burglary and what his father had

said to him about the Farmers' Bank. He was seeking confirmation.

"Well, I can certainly tell you about the Divella case, where the guy got skinned alive by that bank. We handled it. And we conducted an investigation. But, you see, it turns out they were very clever, and Divella was careless. We were unable to come up with any evidence that they used loan-sharking methods, even though we were certain they had. Also, there's another important thing to bear in mind, which is that we were working on our own initiative, because Divella didn't want to press charges."

"Did he fear reprisals?"

"Perhaps."

Montalbano smiled.

"Your 'perhaps' has got me walking in a minefield now."

Now it was Antoci who smiled, but he said nothing.

"Is there a whiff of the Mafia about that bank?" Montalbano asked out of the blue.

Antoci made a serious face.

"Let's say a faint whiff—or rather, the ever-so-slightest, barely perceptible whiff."

A bit like the barber's-salon aroma still wafting about inside the bank's walls.

"Care to explain a little better?"

"The president, the managing director, and the advisers all have clean records and no known connections to the Mafia. They're businessmen, yes, and unscrupulous. But if they're violating the criminal code, as might have been the case with Divella, then . . ."

"And where is this ever-so-slight whiff?"

"It's coming from the office of the general manager, a certain Cesare Gigante, attorney-at-law, who ten years ago married the sister of Memè Laurentano, a Mafia capo with the Sinagra clan. Laurentano's daughter is married to another employee of the same bank, Vittorio Barracuda, who is presently manager of the Vigàta branch."

Montalbano's eyes opened wide.

"Are you serious?"

"Of course I'm serious. But don't get your hopes up. We've been keeping an eye on both Gigante and Barracuda for a good while, and we're not the only ones. Nothing's come up that we could use against them. Stellar conduct, aside from their unfortunate tendency to loan-sharking. But here's an extra detail: The two women have broken off their relationships with their respective brother and father."

When Montalbano got back to the station, Fazio told him that Forensics hadn't found anything, not even the fingerprints of the bank's own employees. Clearly the burglars had used gloves and, just to be safe, had carefully wiped everything down.

The inspector told him about his meeting with Marshal Antoci. Fazio became pensive.

"What is it?"

"I was just wondering who would ever be crazy enough to go and rob a bank managed by Laurentano's son-in-law."

"Couldn't it be some kind of vendetta?" asked the inspector.

"By whom?"

"By someone who was taken to the cleaners by the bank."

"First of all, that wouldn't be vendetta but suicide. And secondly, that burglary was the work of professionals!"

They fell silent. Then Fazio said:

"Oh! I was forgetting something. I scratched around for information and found out something strange."

"And what was that?"

"The bank's central office, in Montelusa, has fifty safety-deposit boxes. Now my question is: Why would the bank's central office have fifty, and the Vigàta branch one hundred?"

"Maybe they wanted to decentralize."

"Okay, but decentralize what?"

"Who knows. You think the DA will get me an injunction to force Barracuda to give me the list of people renting safety-deposit boxes?"

"I wouldn't get my hopes up."

"I'm not. So we need to find some other way."

"How?"

"At the moment I have no idea. But I'll think of something."

Five minutes after Fazio had left, Catarella came in.

"Chief, 'ere'd be a jinnelman onna premisses 'at wants a talk t'yiz poissonally in poisson."

"What's his name?"

"'E says 'is name is Provisorio."

How could anyone have a surname like that?

"Are you sure, Cat?"

"Sure 'bout wha', Chief?"

"That the gentleman's name is Provisorio?"

"Swear to Gad, Chief."

The well-dressed man of about sixty who appeared at the door seemed gentle and well-bred.

"May I? My name is Carmelo Provvisorio."

Montalbano did a double take. How did Catarella finally get somebody's surname right? Was it because it was a very strange name?

"Please come in. What can I do for you?"

"It's about the burglary at the Farmers' Bank."

Montalbano pricked up his ears.

"Who told you there'd been a burglary?"

"Signor Barracuda, the manager, called me to tell me the safety-deposit boxes had been broken into and advised me not to say anything to anyone about it."

"Did you have a box there?"

"Yes."

"Are you a farmer or—"

"No, I'm a pensioner. You see, after they hired my nephew Angelo, who I brought up after he was orphaned at the age of three, as a cashier, at that bank . . . I thought it was my duty to transfer my account there. And I also rented a safety-deposit box to securely store the jewels of my poor wife, Ernestina, who died four years ago."

"So why did you come to us?"

"I brought a list and some photographs of her jewelry, so if you did happen to find them . . ."

"I see. Please wait just one minute."

He rang Fazio, summoned him, and told him who Provvisorio was and what he wanted. The inspector took his leave of the gentleman, who followed Fazio into his office.

Barely five minutes had gone by when an idea flashed in the inspector's brain. He shot to his feet and ran to Fazio's room, throwing the door open wide. The two looked at him in shock.

"Listen, Signor Provvisorio, is your nephew's name also Provvisorio?"

"No, it's Curreli. He's my sister's son."

"What are his working hours at the bank?"

"He's there till seven p.m."

"Could you please do me a favor and call him and ask if he could drop by the station after he gets off work?"

"But Barracuda, the manager, has sent them all home already."

"Why?"

"I really don't know; that's all my nephew told me."

"Well, please call him anyway."

"If I could use your phone . . ."

"Go ahead," said Fazio.

Provvisorio dialed a number.

"'Ngilì? Inspector Montalbano would like to speak with you. Could you come to the police station?"

After hearing the answer, he hung up the phone.

"He'll be here in about twenty minutes."

"Thank you," said Montalbano, returning to his office.

If the nephew was an honest man like his uncle, he may have noticed some things at the bank that didn't quite add up.

Angelo Curreli was the only key they had that might open the armored door hiding the secrets of the hundred deposit boxes.

At least, that was what the inspector was hoping.

4

Angelo Curreli was a shy, polite, and slightly awkward young man of twenty-five, the same one the inspector had seen at the bank staring at a fly in the air. Montalbano sat him down opposite his desk. Fazio was sitting in the other chair.

"Signor Curreli, thank you for coming. Let me start by saying that you should consider this a conversation among friends and feel free not to answer any of my questions if you so decide. All right?"

"All right."

"How is it working at the bank?"

Curreli visibly gave a start.

"How did you know?"

"Signor Curreli, I assure you that I know nothing whatsoever about you."

"I'm sorry, I misunderstood. Since I'd secretly sent my résumé to three different Palermo banks, I thought maybe that . . ."

"So, you're not so happy at the Farmers' Bank? Or am I mistaken?"

"Well, it's not that I'm unhappy. It's just that . . ."

"You want to quit to pursue a career?"

"I want to quit, but not to pursue a career."

"Why, then?"

Angelo squirmed in his chair. It was hard for him to say what he was thinking.

"When a customer with a safety-deposit box comes in, which of you three clerks goes with him into the secure room?" asked Montalbano, to prod him.

"None of us. The manager takes care of it himself."

"And what if the manager isn't there?"

"That's never happened."

"Maybe the customers let him know in advance," Fazio ventured.

"I doubt it," said Curreli.

"Well, you must admit it's a bit frustrating for a client to go to the bank and come out empty-handed," said Montalbano.

Curreli heaved a long sigh and then spoke.

"It was exactly this way of doing things that started arousing my suspicions. So I began to pay attention to what was up with the deposit boxes and I discovered something disturbing. And that's why I want to quit."

"Please tell me what you discovered."

"There are a hundred safety-deposit boxes. Aside from my uncle's box, the other ninety-nine are rented out to ninety-nine different people."

Montalbano felt disappointed. But the young man went on:

"But there are only two people who ever come to open them, always the same two, equipped with power of attorney and keys for all the boxes."

"Always the same two people?"

"Always the same."

"Do you know their names?"

"Yes. Michele Gammacurta and Pasquale Aricò."

Montalbano and Fazio exchanged a quick glance.

"One last favor. When you go into work tomorrow—"

"But I'm not going in tomorrow!"

"Why not?"

"Because the manager told us the branch office will remain closed for at least a week. The accounts have all been transferred temporarily to the Montelusa office."

"Could you give me the home phone numbers of Barracuda, the manager, and the managing director, Gigante?"

"Sure."

He dictated them to Fazio, who wrote them down.

━━━

Fazio returned after showing the young man out. By now it was almost six o'clock. Montalbano put on the speakerphone and dialed the number of the Montelusa headquarters of the Farmers' Bank.

"Hello? This is the Honorable Giovanni Saraceno speaking. Could I speak to Signor Gigante, please?"

"I'm so sorry, sir," said the receptionist. "But Signor Gigante left on holiday just this morning with his family. If you'd like to speak to—"

"No, thank you."

He hung up, then dialed Barracuda's home number. The phone rang a long time, but nobody answered.

"How much you want to bet that he's gone on vacation with his family?"

"I never bet when I'm sure to lose. Since Gammacurta and Aricò are trusted men of the Sinagras, what do you think was in those deposit boxes?"

"Cold cash. Instead of taking it out of the country, which is always risky, they were keeping it here, in a small bank of no importance."

"So the Cuffaros, the Sinagras' sworn enemies, found out and screwed them?"

Montalbano shook his head no.

163

"And why not?" Fazio insisted.

"Look, if it had been the Cuffaros, Barracuda would have been scared out of his wits, because he would have to account for the mishap to the Sinagras. Whereas he was perfectly calm and all smiles."

"So who was it, then?"

"Gammacurta and Aricò."

Fazio very nearly fell out of his chair.

"With Barracuda's complicity, of course, as well as that of the entire Sinagra clan," Montalbano concluded.

"I don't understand anything anymore," said Fazio.

"I'll explain. That money, or at least ninety-nine percent of it, did not belong to the Sinagras, but had been entrusted to them to speculate on. By people with closets full of skeletons—criminals, if not outright mafiosi. But apparently at a certain moment the Sinagras needed the cash and so they set up a burglary, which allowed them to steal the money and still look like victims."

"You may even be right, Chief, but how on earth will we ever prove it?"

"I can't work miracles. We'll wait and see. Listen, I have to go to Montelusa to pick up Livia, who's coming in at six-thirty. I want you to go by Barracuda's house and see if they've gone away. I'll call you later to find out."

The bus was going to be an hour late because the flight had landed an hour late. Montalbano went and sat in a bar and, after letting forty-five minutes go by, rang Fazio.

"What've you got to tell me?"

"You were right on target. A neighbor lady told me the

Barracuda family left in their car around five o'clock, with some suitcases on the roof."

"So it's going to be a long vacation."

"So it would seem. But why, in your opinion?"

"Don't you know Leopardi? They waiting for the calm after the storm."

"You think the people who entrusted their money to the Sinagras are going to remain calm?"

A short while later, the bus finally arrived.

At seven o'clock the following morning, the phone rang, waking up Montalbano, who was sleeping in Livia's arms.

"Mmm," said the young woman, disturbed by the ringing and by Salvo's movements. It was Fazio.

"Chief, can you come to Vicolo Cannarozzo, which is the first side street on the left off Via Cristoforo Colombo? Somebody got shot and killed there."

He didn't bother to inform Livia that he was going out. He would call her later.

In Vicolo Cannarozzo there were two squad cars. Four uniformed cops were keeping the rubberneckers away.

The dead man lay on the sidewalk right in front of the door from which he had apparently just emerged.

"Shot seven times, no less," said Fazio. "By two guys on a motorcycle."

"Did you know this guy?"

"Yeah. His name was Filippo Portera, a small-time mafioso with the Cuffaro family."

And he gave the inspector a meaningful look.

"Are you telling me I was wrong?" Montalbano asked.

"It does look that way."

"So this murder supposedly means that it was the Cuf-faros who robbed the bank and the Sinagras are starting to avenge themselves?"

"C'mon, Chief, what's two plus two? And now I'm wor-ried another war between the two families'll break out. We'd better get ready for the worst."

At that moment two cars pulled up. In the first one was Augello; in the second, Zito the newsman from the Free Channel and a cameraman.

"Salvo, would you do an interview for me?" Zito asked.

"Sure, if you keep it brief."

———

"Inspector Montalbano, do you think this killing marks the beginning of a new war between the Mafias of our town?"

"Every war has a motive that triggers it, usually stem-ming from the desire on the part of one of the two adversar-ies to increase their power. In the present case, in my opinion, there is no triggering motive. This killing is supposed to make us believe that a war is about to break out."

"Could you be a little clearer?"

"This is Pirandello's home turf, isn't it? Appearance and reality. In the present case—only in my opinion, mind you—somebody wants to make something appear a certain way, whereas the reality of that thing is completely different."

"Inspector Montalbano—"

"That'll be enough, thanks."

"But I can't broadcast that!" Zito protested.

"Well, you're gonna broadcast it anyway, and right away. Somebody will understand it."

Montalbano then hurried over to Augello.

"Mimì, you wait here for the prosecutor, Forensics, and everyone else. I'll see you at the office after lunch."

And he raced away, back to Marinella. Livia was still asleep. He got undressed and lay down beside her.

At one o'clock, as Livia was getting dressed to go out with him for lunch at Calogero's, he turned on the television to watch the TeleVigàta news report. Pippo Ragonese, the station's chief reporter and often a willing spokesman for the Mafia, was speaking.

> . . . *and we who have so often criticized the overly nonchalant modus operandi of Inspector Montalbano, this time we cannot help but appreciate his caution and old-fashioned good sense, which—*

He turned it off. The message had been received.

As soon as he got to the office, Fazio assailed him.

"Chief, you have to explain the meaning of that interview to me."

"Did you watch Ragonese?"

"Yeah, but I didn't understand a thing."

"It's quite simple. I let it be known that I'd understood everything. That is, that it was the Sinagras themselves who organized the burglary at their bank and killed Portera to make it look like it had been the Cuffaros. I defused the bomb that was about to explode."

Around four o'clock Fazio came back into Montalbano's office. He looked bewildered.

"Provvisorio called just now—remember him? He says he found a parcel outside his front door with the stolen jewelry in it. What does it mean?"

"That a transaction between the Cuffaros and Sinagras has begun. Part of the stolen money will be returned, and the remainder will be divvied up between the Cuffaros and Sinagras. But I think the transaction contains a few other stipulations."

It was an easy prophecy. Half an hour later, Fazio returned, more bewildered than ever.

"Chief, Michele Gammacurta is dead."

"Shot?"

"No, he was driving his car while drunk and fell into a gully. The strange thing is that Gammacurta didn't drink."

"Nothing strange about that. Apparently the transaction included the stipulation that the person who killed Portera must die. And this is just the opportunity I've been waiting for. Quick, grab a couple of officers and bring me Pasquale Aricò, immediately."

"And if he asks me the reason, what should I tell him?"

"Tell him I want to save his life."

It took him two hours to convince Aricò that he was going to be the next victim, and that this would close out the transaction between the Cuffaros and Sinagras. The stipulation according to which the Cuffaros demanded the death of the two who'd killed Portera had been respected by the Sinagras by arranging the death of Gammacurta. It would be his turn next. Didn't he realize this?

When he finally did realize this, Aricò opened up. And

spilled the beans. All of them: about the Farmers' Bank, the safety-deposit boxes, Barracuda, Gigante . . .

The inspector rang Livia and told her he'd be a little late. Then, with Fazio at the wheel, he took Aricò to the prosecutor's office in Montelusa.

He wanted to get things over with quickly, so he could race back home, where Livia was waiting for him.

STANDARD PROCEDURE

1

Even though Montalbano's face was known to everyone and his dog, he had managed, at long last, with a word here and a word there, to weasel his way into an auction. Two people had come to fetch him at home at midnight, and by one o'clock they arrived at a farm estate way out in the country that would have looked uninhabited if not for the thirty-odd cars and two vans parked in the general area. He was led into a large warehouse. There were some forty chairs already almost completely occupied in front of a dais lit up by large floodlights. Behind the podium was a small, closed door.

For Montalbano they'd reserved a front-row seat between a gaunt man of about forty and a fiftyish man as fat as a barrel. The skinny man, a big-time businessman by the name of Giliberto who knew the inspector, reacted with surprise.

"You, here?"

"Well!" said Montalbano, throwing up his hands in resignation, as if to say that he, too, suffered from the weakness of the flesh.

The door behind the podium opened and a man appeared, dressed exactly the way the guardians of harems used to dress, with a turban and pointy babouches.

"Gentlemen, the auction is hereby open!" he said, in the voice of a strangled rooster.

A eunuch, perhaps? So the story about them cutting the the balls off the harem guards was true after all?

"The first absolutely priceless item I have the honor of presenting to you tonight," the eunuch continued, "is a Moldavian girl who has just turned nineteen, Ekaterina Smirnova. She was imported directly by our organization, and therefore we can guarantee that she is almost entirely new merchandise."

He then assumed a sly expression.

"She has tremendous linguistic ability. Ah, but don't get the wrong idea. Ekaterina speaks and writes five languages fluently. The bidding will begin at one hundred and fifty thousand lire."

A very young girl walked in, blond as the sun, completely naked and smiling, and exhibited herself to the crowd, first the front, then the back, after which she began a sort of dance, lying down on the floor and spreading her legs and then getting up on all fours.

Montalbano felt a little confused. A hundred and fifty thousand lire for a beautiful girl like that seemed very little to him.

"The starting price seems a little low to me," he said to Giliberto.

"Well," Giliberto explained, "the problem is not the acquisition price, you see; the real problem is the cost of maintenance. The more beautiful the girls, the more expensive their daily upkeep: hairdresser, beautician, manicurist, masseur . . . Then there's the wardrobe, which must be top-drawer, and the options, such as necklaces, bracelets . . . Then there's also the apartment, the restaurant costs . . . Those are major expenses, you know."

Meanwhile the girl had been sold to the owner of a fishing trawler for two hundred thousand lire.

"I'm sorry," Montalbano insisted. "But what do you do when you start to get tired of her?"

"You bring her back to the organization," said Giliberto, "and they make her work the streets."

"And what if the girl refuses?"

"That's unlikely. But if that happens, they scrap her."

Now it was the turn of a dark, sinuous twenty-year-old girl, with a body you had to see to believe. With every move she made she appeared to be dancing.

"The bidding will start at two hundred thousand," said the eunuch.

"Two hundred and fifty thousand," said Montalbano, acting out the role he'd been assigned.

"Two hundred and fifty thousand lire. Going once," said the eunuch.

Nobody said anything.

"Anybody care to make another offer? Look at those aerodynamic breasts! Admire the bold curve of those buttocks!"

Chaste but efficient in his pitch, that eunuch.

"Don't be shy! No other offers? Okay. Two hundred and fifty thousand lire, going twice."

Nobody said anything this time, either.

"No other offers? Then, sold! For two hundred and fifty thousand lire!"

Montalbano's blood froze. He'd bought himself a woman! A sex slave! What the hell was he going to tell Livia?

At that moment a telephone rang.

"It's for you," the eunuch said to Montalbano. "Go and answer!"

How could he know? Flummoxed, Montalbano stood up and then woke up. The telephone was still ringing. He breathed a sigh of relief. So he hadn't bought himself a woman, he'd just dreamt it. He looked at the clock. Six-thirty in the morning. He got out of bed and answered the phone.

"Iss terribly imbarrassin' an' I beckon you a towzan' partin's, Chief, f' callin' yiz so oily inna morninlike. Wha' was ya doin', Chief, sleepin'?"

"No, I was playing rugby," Montalbano replied darkly.

"I nevveh unnastood nuttin' 'bout that."

"About what?"

"'Bout that 'Murcan game you was playin'."

"Cat, you wanna tell me why you called me?"

"'Ere was a hummicide, Chief."

"Explain."

"'Ey foun' a copse o' the fimminine sex inna doorways on Via Pintacucuda, nummer eighteen. Fazio's awreddy onna scene."

"Okay, I'm on my way."

Fazio had taken measures to ensure that rubberneckers were kept a good distance away. The victim was a pretty young woman of about twenty, blond. All she was wearing was a terry-cloth bathrobe, which in her fall had come open, revealing that she'd been cut with a blade all over her body. Little cuts, both deep and superficial, from her throat to her feet. There wasn't much blood.

"They didn't kill her here," said Montalbano.

"Certainly not," said Fazio.

"But it was she herself, despite being half-dead, who'd made it to this spot on her own strength."

"How do you know that?"

"Come with me."

He followed him out of the doorway.

"Look down on the ground."

There were large, dark bloodstains. They led to a blue Suzuki with its driver's-side door half-open.

"Look inside."

Montalbano looked. The driver's seat was all covered in blood. The steering wheel likewise.

"After she was all cut up," Fazio went on, "she had the strength to get in her car, drive here, cross the street, open the front door—the key is still in the lock—and go inside. But she didn't make it any farther. She'd lost too much blood."

They went back into the doorway.

"Who discovered her?"

"A certain Michele Tarantino, who was coming out of the building at six, on his way to work."

"Where is he now?"

"He's in his apartment. Second floor, number six."

"I'm going to go and talk to him. Have you alerted the circus? Forensics, DA, Pasquano?"

"Already taken care of."

There was no elevator. He climbed the stairs, knocked, and the door was opened by an enormous woman with a waistline of at least twelve feet and arms capable of snapping the inspector in two without breaking a sweat.

"What the hell is it now?"

"It's Inspector Montalbano."

"What the fuck do I care?"

Montalbano forced himself to stuff it.

"I would like to speak with Signor Michele Tarantino."

"Signor Michele, as you call him, is in the toilet vomiting. That's all he's been doing since he found the dead body. My husband's a sensitive man!"

She let the inspector in, then howled:

"Michè! C'm 'ere! There's somebody here to bust your balls again!"

And she walked away, muttering to herself. Michele Tarantino was a tiny, skinny man of about fifty, and if he was two inches shorter you could have legitimately called him a midget.

"Tell me something, sir. When you saw the girl, was she still alive or already dead?"

"No, she was already dead."

The man must have been from Catania, to judge from his accent.

"And what did you do?"

"Me? I didn't do nothing. I just started vomiting."

"But then who was it that called us?"

"Signor Aurelio Scarmacca, who lives just across the landing from us, and who turned up at the exact same moment."

"Was he on his way out, too?"

"No, he was coming home. He works as a night watchman."

"And what did you do?"

"I came upstairs to throw up."

"Had you ever seen the girl before?"

"Never. She didn't live here."

Aurelio Scarmacca had wisely not gone to bed. He was keeping himself awake by dint of coffee.

"Would you like some, too, sir?"

"Sure, why not? Thank you."

Serving the coffee was Scarmacca's wife, Signora Ciccina.

"Signor Scarmacca, how did you get inside? Did you use the key that—"

"That's exactly right," said Scarmacca, a smart fellow of about forty. "I saw the key in the lock and—"

"I'm sorry, but was there only that one key in the lock? It wasn't part of a set?"

"No, it was all by itself."

"Okay, go on."

"I figured one of the tenants must have forgotten it there, so I turned it and went in, and then I saw the body and Signor Tarantino, who was trembling. And so I closed the front door, came upstairs to our flat, called you on the phone, went back downstairs, and opened the front door halfway—I'm always the one who opens it in the morning—so that you couldn't see the body from the street. And then I stood guard and waited there until the police arrived."

"You did the right thing. But, tell me, had you ever seen the girl before?"

"No, sir."

"She didn't live here," Signora Ciccina added firmly.

"How can you say that if you haven't seen her?"

"But I did see her. I overheard Aurelio talking on the phone and I went down to look. Not only did she not live here, but I'd never seen her before."

"But she had the key to the outside door," said Montalbano.

"Maybe she came at night, in secret, when everyone was asleep," said Signora Ciccina.

"And what would she come here for at night?"

"What do you think a pretty girl's gonna come here for at night? It doesn't take a lot of imagination!"

"And who was she coming to see, in your opinion?"

"Ah, don't ask me. I never spied on nobody in my life," said Signora Ciccina, hardening her face.

Best give her a wide berth.

"How many floors are there in this building?"

"Six. Four apartments per floor."

"Are there any bachelors living in any?"

"Yessir. There's Signor Guarnotta, and there's Signor Ballassare on the fifth floor."

"All right, then. Thank you for your cooperation," said Montalbano, standing up.

"Then," Signora Ciccina continued, "there are two apartments rented to two girls—one is Signorina Gioeli, and the other's name is Persico. If it's all right with you, I can go and talk to these two women."

"Why would you want to do that?"

"Because nobody can ever really say that a man's a man and a woman's a woman when it comes to going to bed. Know what I mean?"

He knew exactly what she meant.

He went downstairs. None of the circus had shown up yet.

"Apparently the girl didn't live here," he said to Fazio. "Listen, I'm going back to the office. This afternoon— starting at three-thirty—I want to see Signor Guarnotta and Signor Ballassare, and two young women, surnames Gioeli and Persico, all of whom live in this building. And one more thing. It's possible the girl who was killed had another key, for her own apartment. Have them search carefully in her car, under the body, anywhere they can. See you later."

2

After eating he got back to the office just before three-thirty and found Fazio waiting for him. His assistant handed him a key.

"So you found it!"

"No, Chief, I didn't. That's the front-door key. Forensics was unable to get any clear fingerprints from it. But I also got two photos of the girl."

He set them down on the desk and said:

"The two women are already here, you know."

"Tell Catarella to bring the first one in, and then come back here."

Albertina Gioeli was wearing clothes that made her look like a cross between a women's-reformatory guard and a nun. She was about thirty and fat, and had a mustache.

"I sent for Don Celestino to bless the building's entrance," she informed the inspector as soon as she sat down. "I'm also making a collection to pay the priest to say four Masses for the soul of that poor girl who was murdered. Would you like to contribute?"

Caught off-guard, Montalbano made a contribution.

"Had you ever seen this girl?" he asked her, showing her one of the photos.

"Never!"

The inspector saw no point in continuing. This woman was not the kind to receive another woman at night. Graziella Persico was instead another matter altogether. A pretty, well-groomed twenty-five-year-old with long legs and wearing a miniskirt, she worked as a secretary for Arlotta, a notary, and had never seen the victim before, either. For no apparent reason, Montalbano fired a shot in the dark.

"You live on the sixth floor, correct? I have to tell you that at least two of your fellow female tenants, one from the second floor and the other on the fourth, told me that sometimes, at night, they'd . . ."

And he stopped there, because he couldn't come up quick enough with what the two fellow female tenants might have told him. Luckily, however, Graziella turned red as a beet.

"I'm certainly not doing anything wrong. I'm a legal adult, I have no boyfriend, I am absolutely free. So, if Pippinello . . . I mean Signor Arlotta, the notary, comes to see me every now and then . . . He's a very unhappy man, you know? His wife has never—"

"That'll be all, thank you," Montalbano interrupted her, dismissing her at once.

At first glance, and also at second and third glance, *ragioniere* Ballassare didn't seem the type who would be having girls over for the night. He looked about fifty, was impeccably dressed all in black, and had the unsavory air of someone who was born an orphan, was always depressed, and sapped the will to live of anyone who came near him.

He'd never seen the slain girl before.

"Tell me something, *ragioniere*. What do you do for a living?"

"I'm a bookkeeper at a funeral home."

He certainly wasn't trying to mislead anyone with his appearance.

Davide Guarnotta shook the inspector's hand as he came in and smiled at Fazio. He was a handsome young man of about thirty, with black hair and eyes, likable and open.

"Do you two know each other?" asked Montalbano.

"Signor Guarnotta didn't sleep at home last night," Fazio explained. "He came home around eight o'clock this morning, but our men wouldn't let him in, so I intervened and we set everything straight."

"Just to make sure I wasn't a journalist, he came with me and stayed with me until I opened my front door," said Guarnotta.

"May I ask you why you didn't sleep at home last night?" asked Montalbano.

"Can't you imagine?" Guarnotta asked in turn, grinning.

"Haven't you ever slept at home with another person?"

"A few times, but not often."

"Why not?"

"Because I'm jealously protective of my things. It would bother me, for example, to have a woman rifling through my photos."

"Are you a photographer?"

"No, I'm a freelance cameraman. I often work for Tele-Vigàta. Photography's just a hobby."

"Have you ever seen this girl?"

Guarnotta picked up the photograph and looked at it long and hard. Then he shook his head.

"No, never. But she does look a lot like a Russian girl I know."

"Are you sure it's not her?"

"Absolutely."

After dismissing Guarnotta, Montalbano and Fazio sat for a few minutes looking at each other in silence. Then Fazio said:

"It's gonna be hard to identify her."

"Take one of the photos and show it to everyone in the building," said the inspector. "Starting now. Though I think it'll probably be useless. The only hope is that Dr. Pasquano might be able to tell us something after the autopsy. But he's going to take his time. I doubt we'll hear from him for another three or four days."

After Fazio left, the inspector summoned Catarella.

"Take this photo and see if it matches any missing persons' reports."

"Straightaways, Chief."

Later, as the inspector was leaving the office to go home, Catarella gave the photo back to him and informed him that none of the girls portrayed in the missing persons' reports looked at all like the murder victim.

The following morning Fazio reported that of all the tenants in the building, only one person, a woman, upon seeing the girl's photo, claimed to have seen her before. Nobody else recognized her.

"What's this lady's name?"

"Adele Manfredonio. She's eighty years old, has a husband who's paralyzed, and she lives on the third floor."

"Eighty years old? But can she still see properly?"

"Her vision is perfect, Chief, and she wanted to prove it to me by reading the newspaper headlines from five steps away."

"And when did she supposedly see her?"

"One night last month around two o'clock in the morning, as she was opening her front door. After opening it, she went out onto the landing and saw the girl, who was starting to climb the stairs leading to the floor above."

"Wait a second. How did she see her face?"

"When the girl heard a noise, she stopped and turned around. The lady says the girl even smiled at her."

"Can you tell me exactly what the old lady was doing out on the landing at two o'clock in the morning?"

"She was looking for her cat, who sometimes escapes and doesn't come home till late."

Montalbano thought of something.

"Remember what Guarnotta told us? That he had a Russian girlfriend who looked like the victim? Let's check that out. Get me Guarnotta on the phone and then put me on."

Five minutes later he had the young man on the line. Montalbano turned on the speakerphone.

"Sorry to bother you, but I'd like you to answer an important question. About a month ago, did that Russian girlfriend of yours—the one who looks like the murder victim—did she come to your place during the night?"

"Natasha? Yes. She came again about a week ago as well, as far as that goes. She dropped by to say good-bye."

"She went away?"

"She went back to St. Petersburg. Suddenly felt homesick. She'll be back in a month."

"So," said Montalbano, after closing the communication, "the person Signora Manfredonio saw was definitely Natasha."

"I agree," said Fazio. "But a big question remains, so big you can't see past it: Why did the girl have a key to the front door?"

At around eleven o'clock that same morning Montalbano tried something. He phoned the Institute for Forensic Medicine and asked for Dr. Pasquano. He imagined they would tell him to call back, but they actually put him on right away.

"How come you're not working, Doctor?"

"Why, do I have to answer to you or something? But if you really must know, I was taking a short break to go to the toilet. Doesn't that ever happen to you? Or do you prefer doing it in your pants? And do you mind telling me why the hell you're busting my chops at this hour of the morning?"

"I just wanted to know if you had anything to tell me about the girl who was stabbed to death."

"Just be patient and wait for the report."

"Can't you give me a little preview?"

"For a price."

"Shall we say six cannoli?"

"Make it ten and you've got a deal."

He stopped at the Caffè Castiglione, ordered a tray of ten cannoli, got back in his car, and headed for Montelusa. The first thing Pasquano did upon greeting him was eat one cannolo. The second thing he did was eat another. Then he looked at Montalbano and asked:

"What do you want to know?"

"Anything you can tell me."

"First of all, she was very young, not even twenty, if you ask me. Body in excellent shape. To judge from some dental work she had done, I would assume she was from an Eastern European country. She had been raped repeatedly by several men and in every way possible and imaginable. Then they bound her wrists and hung her from some sort of hook—the marks are quite visible—and they started torturing her systematically."

Montalbano turned pale. Pasquano noticed.

"What, does that upset you? We're off to a good start! What should we do?"

"Would you please continue?" the inspector said brusquely.

"My, aren't we touchy! Yessiree, tortured for hours on end, inflicting cuts to every part of the body, with a very sharp dagger. The cuts then started getting deeper, and when they thought they'd killed her, they untied the rope around her wrists and left her there on the floor. I'm sure they were going to come back to get rid of the body. But the girl—who I told you was in superb physical shape—regained consciousness, managed to get outside, climb into her car, and get as far as Via Pintacuda. There were traces of grass and asphalt on the soles of her feet. And there you have it, my good man. Would you like to join me for a cannolo?"

Montalbano shook his head no. His stomach was in knots.

"Why do you think they tortured her?"

"She was probably part of some criminal gang and either betrayed them or refused to tell them something that only she knew. Oh, and one more detail. To keep her from screaming, they stuffed her bra into her mouth. She swallowed the hook."

He recounted to Fazio what Pasquano had told him. Fazio looked doubtful.

"What is it you're not convinced about?"

"The bit about the girl being part of some criminal gang."

"Why?"

"Chief, in the condition she was in, it's not as if the girl could have driven very far in her car. This is something that happened in Vigàta or nearby. So where are these criminal gangs? With that kind of ferocity? And it can't be a Mafia thing, either, because the Mafia doesn't act that way."

"I agree with you."

"So what do you think this is about?"

"Exploitation and prostitution."

"What do you mean?"

"Even in Vigàta we've got a fair number of foreign girls imported to work as prostitutes. And their pimps can be quite ferocious with any one of them that slips up. They have to set an example. The fact that they gang-raped her seems to me rather indicative of this."

"You may be right."

"But if that's the way it is, there is something we can do. This commerce in young flesh can only be practiced with the consent of the Mafia. Who probably even take a cut."

"That's true."

"You need to inform yourself. Who is associated with that circuit? The Cuffaros or the Sinagras? If we knew that, it would be a good start."

"I'll start asking around today."

"Yes, because . . ."

"Because?"

"Because a murder so atrocious, so ruthless, preceded by long hours of torture, is probably not to the Mafia's liking, either, or not to the liking of part of the Mafia. Actually, you know what I say? This afternoon, I'm going to have Zito interview me. Give me back the girl's picture."

Nicolò Zito, the news editor of the Free Channel, who was a close friend of Montalbano's, interrupted the filming.

"I'm sorry, Salvo, but the way the interview's turning out, I can't possibly broadcast it. You're too crude in your description of the details. It sounds like a horror movie. Try to soften it a little."

"Unfortunately it's not a movie. And that's exactly what I want people to feel: horror. But I'll try and soften it a little."

They did it over.

3

". . . and despite the fact that the tortures she'd been subjected to had reduced her to a mass of bleeding flesh, the poor girl found the strength to get into her car, drive a certain distance, open the front door in Via Pintacuda, and go inside. But then she fell to the floor and breathed her last."

"Did she know anyone in Via Pintacuda?"

"None of the tenants has admitted to knowing her. But the girl had in her possession a key to the front door. Someone must have given it to her."

"But did she also have the key to one of the apartments in the building?"

"We don't know. We didn't find any."

"What do you think the motive could be?"

"A tragic, indeed a perverse show of power."

"Could you explain a little?"

"No, no more questions, please."

Zito signaled to the cameraman to stop filming.

"What kind of way is that to end an interview? Your answer didn't say a goddamn thing!" he protested.

"It didn't say anything to you, but somebody else will get the message. I can't be any clearer because I, too, can only make conjectures. Between you and me, I can tell you I think it was the work of some prostitution ring. The girl probably rebelled, and they wanted to make an example of her, to show the others what they are capable of. But I'm telling you, Nicolò: I want you to broadcast the girl's picture repeatedly and say that anyone who recognizes her should immediately contact the police or your station."

———

After leaving the Free Channel studios, which were in Montelusa, the inspector coasted ever so slowly back down to Vigàta. He stayed in his office for a couple of hours signing useless documents, then went home early, because he wanted to watch the eight o'clock evening news. And indeed, despite the fact that he had softened somewhat his description of the rape and the torture, the interview inspired horror and dismay. When it was over he set the table out on the veranda and feasted on the *pasta 'ncasciata* that Adelina, his housekeeper, had made for him. At ten o'clock he turned the TV back on. Nicolò Zito was saying that they had received dozens of phone calls from indignant people saying they wanted to see the killers thrown in jail as soon as possible. He also said that two men thought they recognized the girl. But he added no more on the subject. The broadcast had just finished when the telephone rang.

"I want to tell you about those two phone calls," said Zito.

"Were they anonymous?"

"Yes. Two men. They both said the same thing: that the girl, whose name they didn't know, dealt drugs at the Labrador."

The Labrador was a huge nightclub with two dance floors. One of them was the realm of youngsters of both sexes; the other was much smaller and had all the features of an exclusive "gentlemen's club." Everyone knew the place was owned by the Cuffaro family.

This was undoubtedly interesting news. At midnight the inspector watched the late-night news report of TeleVigàta, the main competitor of the Free Channel and a progovernment station that was not above occasionally giving a little under-the-table boost to the Mafia. Pippo Ragonese, their top newsman, was interviewing a stocky, well-dressed man of about fifty with a mustache.

189

"You, Signor Lacuccia, are the manager of the Labrador, are you not?"

"Yes, for the past year."

"Have you heard the persistent rumor that the recently murdered girl was someone who sold drugs at your establishment?"

"Yes, I have."

"Have you seen the photo of the murdered girl that was broadcast on the news?"

"Yes, I have."

"What can you tell us about her?"

"All I know is the girl's first name, Vera, and I can say that she did, for a while, frequent our establishment, but then I ordered the doormen not to let her in anymore."

"Why not?"

"Because I'd gotten wind that she was dealing drugs. That's something I do not tolerate in my nightclub."

"Would she come alone or with company?"

"She would come with whoever she could find."

"So you assume that her murder was the result of some settling of accounts among drug dealers?"

"I think that's pretty clear."

Montalbano turned off the set and went to bed.

———

"Ahh, Chief, Chief! Ah, Chief!" Catarella said the following morning as soon as the inspector walked in.

This litany of lament meant that Hizzoner the C'mishner of P'leece had called.

"What did he want?"

"'E says as how ya gotta call 'im, 'im bein' 'Izzoner the C'mishner, straightawayslike and all emoigently emoigentlike."

"Okay."

Montalbano went into his office, sat down, and rang the commissioner.

"Montalbano? I saw your interview on the television last night. A little crude, don't you think?"

"Well, I was trying to—"

"Yes, I gathered that. At any rate, I wanted to tell you in advance that the prosecutor's office has decided to turn the case over to the narcotics unit. And you will do me the favor, if asked, to cooperate with Inspector Gianquinto on the investigation. And just for your information, the prefect has taken the measure of shutting down the Labrador for fifteen days. This will be announced sometime this afternoon."

The inspector thanked him and hung up. Then he summoned Fazio and informed him of the phone conversation he'd just had.

"So what are we gonna do?"

"We're gonna go right ahead and fuck 'em all. I have to cooperate anyway, so why not? Got any news?"

"Yeah. The local prostitution circuit is controlled by two Slavs who nevertheless have to report to the Cuffaros."

"And who's in charge of drugs?"

"The Cuffaros. The Sinagras' fortunes have been in decline lately."

"And these same Cuffaros also own the Labrador."

"What's that got to do with it?"

"Lots. Did you watch the interview with the manager of the Labrador?"

191

"Yes."

"The whole thing was a smokescreen. A red herring the prosecutor's office swallowed whole. The Cuffaros are taking a huge risk by diverting the investigation towards narcotics. Does anyone really believe an employee of the Cuffaros would publicly admit that drugs were being dealt at his establishment? Leading to the club's closing for fifteen days? If he did so, it's because he was ordered to, by the Cuffaros. Which means that there's something else underlying the girl's murder, something huge, something that must by all means remain hidden."

"I told the prosecutor that I was unconvinced by the story of a settling of accounts, but he just dug in his heels," said Gianquinto. "Normally drug dealers settle their differences with a burst of machine-gun fire and that's the end of that. They don't waste their time with rape, torture, and stuff like that."

Gianquinto had shown up at the station as Montalbano was on his way to lunch, and since he seemed like a nice guy, the inspector had invited him to Calogero's.

"These mullet are outstanding," said Gianquinto. "So, tell me what you think."

Montalbano told him. Gianquinto seemed convinced.

"So, how should we proceed?" he asked.

"I think I know a way. So, the Cuffaros want us to think it's about drugs? Fine. We'll pretend we believe them. We'll do them a little damage and see whether the game is still worth the candle to them."

"Explain what you mean."

"Well, if I were you, I would go immediately and do a big-time search of the Labrador. You're sure to find something. They won't have had time to remove everything. That will extend the closure beyond the fifteen days to an indefinite amount of time, and the revenue lost by the Cuffaros will become huge. Then, always assuming you find some stuff, you'll hold a nice press conference and announce that you steadfastly intend to continue down this path."

"Excellent idea," said Gianquinto. "I'll get moving as soon as we're done here."

Gianquinto got back in touch at eight o'clock that evening. He was excited and spoke in dialect.

"You been talking to crows or something?"

"Was I right?"

"Right on the money! In the manager's office—that is, the office of the man who didn't tolerate drugs in his establishment—we found a good bit of heroin, cocaine, and various chemical junk in a hollowed-out leg of his desk!"

"And where was the manager during all this?"

"C'mon, Montalbà, I wasn't born yesterday. He was present for the search, and there was even one of his bodyguards. Nobody can accuse us of planting the stuff ourselves."

"So when's the press conference?"

"Tomorrow morning at eleven."

Montalbano watched the Free Channel's rebroadcast of the press conference the following day at one p.m., from his table at Calogero's, while eating lunch. At a certain point

193

Gianquinto was chivalrous enough to thank his colleague, Montalbano, for his advice in the case. But he didn't reveal what Montalbano had said.

"Chief, how much do you think a freelance cameraman would normally make?" Fazio asked.

Montalbano gave him a confused look.

"How the hell should I know? Why do you ask?"

"Well, Davide Guarnotta, in addition to the Renault he usually drives around, owns a spanking hot Ferrari. Not to mention a nice little forty-foot boat he sometimes takes out on cruises."

"Have you been investigating him?"

"Yeah."

"Why?"

"He's the only person in the building who could have given the girl the key."

There was certainly no doubt about that.

"Maybe he has family money."

"Chief, his dad was a street sweeper and his mother a cleaning lady. Good people, mind you, but penniless."

"We should find out what bank—"

"Already taken care of. I have a friend at the Credito Siciliano. He made it clear that our friend Guarnotta's got a lot of money."

"So where does he get it?"

"That's the big question."

A sudden boom sent the inspector flying out of his chair and Fazio falling into a crouch. It was the door crashing against the wall.

"I'm rilly sorry, jinnelmen, but my 'and slipped," Catarella said from the doorway.

One of these days I'm going to shoot him, thought Montalbano.

But all he said was:

"What is it?"

"An invilope jest arrived f'yiz," said Catarella, stepping forward and setting the envelope down on the desk.

It was a linen envelope with no address or return address.

"Who delivered it?"

"A man," said Catarella.

"Ah, really?!" said Montalbano, feigning surprise. "A man? Are you sure? It wasn't a crustacean or a three-toed sloth?"

"Nah, Chief, I c'n swear to that. 'Zs jest a man, shoily an' soitanly."

"Get the hell outta here!" the inspector exploded.

Montalbano opened the envelope. It contained a VHS cassette and nothing else.

"If you want to watch it right away," said Fazio, "there's a videocassette player in Augello's office."

"Speaking of whom, when's he getting back from his leave?"

"In a week."

They went to Mimì's office and sat down behind the desk, and Fazio set the tape going.

Credits to a silent film called *A Boundless Love* appeared on the screen. It was Italian, and a rarity. It must have been a good seventy years old, or not much less. The images were faded, and the actors looked like ghosts.

After a few minutes of this, Montalbano couldn't take any more and stood up.

"I don't have time to waste on this bullshit," he said.

"Wait a second," said Fazio. "I don't think this film is so easy to find at a video rental shop."

"So what?"

"Did you know that one of Cuffaro's nephews, by the name of Carmelo Tito, is a well-known collector of silent movies?"

Montalbano immediately sat back down. The film told the story of the love between a strong and handsome wood-cutter and the beautiful young wife of the richest man in town, an ugly old codger who lived in a great house at the edge of the forest. The woodcutter and the girl exchange a great many furtive glances and yearn for each other from afar. Then opportunity arrives. The old man tells his wife he will be out all night making merry with his friends. So the girl sends her trusted chambermaid to inform the woodcutter, who at a prearranged hour slips into the great house, and at last the two can spend a night of love together.

Meanwhile the old man, who is getting drunk with some twenty people, between friends and whores, decides to invite everyone to his house. When the two lovers hear voices approaching, they realize they are lost. So the woodcutter tells the girl to cry out, "Help! Thief!" and jumps out the window. They all rush after him in hot pursuit. At a certain point in his flight, however, the woodcutter steps into a trap. To save the girl's honor, taking the axe he carries in his belt, he chops off his foot with one blow and drags himself to the edge of a deep lake. But when he realizes his pursuers are about to catch up with him, he throws himself into the lake, killing himself. And since his body will never be found, everyone will believe that it was a thief who had entered the young wife's bedroom.

4

"Did you understand the deeper meaning?" Montalbano asked Fazio when it was over.

"In part," Fazio replied. "Why don't you explain it a little better to me?"

"This is a reply to Gianquinto's press conference. The Cuffaros are telling me, first of all, that they fully realize that it was I who was behind the closure of the Labrador. And secondly, they're saying that they're not only ready to cut off one foot—that is, to shut down the Labrador for good—but also to lose something even more valuable rather than let someone be publicly shamed. In short, they're telling me they can't act otherwise, that this is a very big deal over which they're prepared to lose men and money."

"And they're saying something else, too," said Fazio.

"And what's that?"

"That in a deal as big as this, you, too, have to cover your rear."

"Yeah, I got that. As I was watching the movie, I started thinking about Davide Guarnotta. You were probably right when you said the only person who could have given the murdered girl the key to the building was none other than Guarnotta. It's possible the asshole is taking us for a ride. It's possible the Russian girlfriend who looks so much like the victim doesn't even exist, and he invented her on the spot. Maybe it was the victim herself who used to go and visit him in the middle of the night. Let's put the screws to him. Start looking for him and find out where he is."

After making a number of phone calls, Fazio was able to talk to Guarnotta.

"He's working at the TeleVigàta studios and will be busy until eight o'clock."

"Perfect. It's six-thirty now. I want you to go to TeleVigàta immediately with two uniformed cops in a squad car with sirens blaring. You have to make a lot of noise, create some confusion. Even if they're filming, just burst in and interrupt them anyway. As if you were going to arrest him. Then tell him I'll be waiting for him at the office at nine o'clock tomorrow morning. And you must threaten him, saying he has no choice but to appear."

"And then what?"

"And then I go home. Be seein' ya."

He had just woken up a few minutes before seven when the phone rang. It was Fazio.

"Chief, about an hour ago somebody called in to report that a car had been found on the western beach with a dead body inside, and I went to check it out. It was Guarnotta. I'm here at the scene and have already alerted the circus. Are you coming?"

"What good would that do? But how did he die?"

"I haven't opened the car. There's no visible injury, no blood. He's in shirtsleeves, leaning back in the driver's seat, head thrown back, eyes bulging . . . Next to his feet on the floor is an elastic and a syringe. Maybe an overdose."

"How did he react yesterday when you informed him I was summoning him to the station?"

"He turned pale, Chief, and just said, 'Okay.'"

"As soon as you're done there, come to the office."

For whatever reason, the death of Guarnotta weighed on the inspector's conscience.

"Chief, somebuddy jess call' sayin' as how durin' the night—'at'd be lass night, bein' at night durin' the night o' yesterday—'ere was a boiglery."

"Where?"

"Same place azza moider: Via Pintacucuda, nummer eighteen. A' Signor Guarnotti's place."

Montalbano shot out of the office like a rocket, grabbed his car, and raced to Via Pintacuda. None of the tenants knew yet about the cameraman's death. And Montalbano didn't inform them. The person who'd noticed that thieves had entered his apartment was Signora Oliveri, who lived across the landing from him.

"When I's on my way out I saw the door was open, an' so I went over an' called out Signor Guarnotta's name, but there was no answer. So I went in and saw that the place had been turned upside down."

The first thing Montalbano noticed was two keys on a ring lying on the floor at the front of the entranceway. He tried one in the door, and it worked. The other must have been to the front door of the building. The thieves had entered using the keys they took off Guarnotta's corpse. Hanging from a nail on the doorjamb was another key. Montalbano took it and tried it. It was the extra key. And so the extra key to the front door was missing. What's two plus two? The key the murdered girl had used clearly belonged to Guarnotta. There could be no doubt.

Photos of naked women stuck on the walls were the apartment's only embellishments. There was also a television set equipped with a videocassette player and a large screen on the wall. Beside it was a small article of furniture that must have once held the hundred or more porno film cassettes that were now strewn across the floor, as if they'd been checked one by one. It didn't take long for Montalbano to become convinced that he wasn't looking at a burglary. Neither the videocassette player nor the costly cameras, nor the television, had been stolen. Actually, what the intruders had done was perform a professional-quality search of the whole flat. There wasn't a single nook or cranny that hadn't been rifled through.

Head filled with thoughts, Montalbano went back to the office. Upon arriving he told Catarella he didn't want to be disturbed by anyone. Nobody but Fazio could come into his office, when he returned.

The inspector sat there a long time, thinking. What does one go looking for in the home of a freelance cameraman? Something that has something to do with his job. In other words, some sort of video recording. Of something compromising. He thought again of the silent film. Something that would compromise certain people who at all costs had to remain above suspicion . . . A thought flashed through his brain like lightning. *Wait a second, Montalbà.* What if it was Guarnotta himself who, as a cameraman, had shot some scene that would become dangerous if put into circulation? And what if he'd made copies of it? Maybe even to use as blackmail? And maybe this was something he'd been doing for a while? Blackmailing, that is. That would explain where the money came from. But what could he have filmed that was so dangerous that the Cuffaros were ready to pay so much to keep it secret? The moment when some honorable parliamentarian was putting a bribe directly into his pocket? Still, the honorable deputy could have wriggled out by saying the money was for some charitable organization. And so? For a second the dream he'd had flashed through his mind. Of course, if he'd filmed a politician buying a woman at the sex-slave market and it came to be known that those same women were later slated for "scrapping," the whole thing would have another significance. Scrapping? What exactly did that mean, anyway? The answer that came to mind made him shudder. And what if those girls were "scrapped" in front of people who liked to see a beautiful girl get "scrapped"? And who paid astronomical sums to witness the spectacle? And what if they even participated in the "scrapping"? And what if the scene was filmed and all present were entitled to a free copy? No, that would be too . . . too . . . His brain didn't want to accept it . . . "A tragic, indeed a perverse show of power," he'd said during the interview. He hadn't, at the time, been able to explain those words to himself. They'd come out by themselves, spontaneously. But they were perfect.

At that moment Fazio walked in.

"Dr. Pasquano immediately declared that Guarnotta was 'suicided' with an overdose. He said it in front of the journalists. You can imagine the splash that'll make!"

"How can he be so sure?"

"Because there was no trace of any puncture wounds other than the one that killed him. And because there were bruises on his arms and legs, a sign that he was being held down by force as they were injecting him."

"Do you remember how in the film they had the guy commit suicide in the lake?"

"You're right. Oh, and I also wanted to tell you that they found nothing personal in the car, not even Guarnotta's house keys."

"The keys were taken by the killers so they could go and search his apartment. I have them myself now: Here they are. I'm also almost certain that it was Guarnotta who gave the key to the girl."

Fazio gave him a puzzled look. Montalbano told him about the burglary and the extra set of keys that was missing the one to the front door.

The telephone rang.

"Chief, 'ere'd a happen a be a jinnelman present 'ere in poisson 'oose name I ferget assept 'at 'e's got one o' the names o' the Tree Kings," said Catarella.

"Melchiorre?" Montalbano suggested.

"'Ass it!"

"Okay, send him in."

Actually it was one of the other Three Kings. *Ragioniere* Ballassare, in fact, the one from the funeral home. He looked even a little more disconsolate than usual.

"I saw about poor Guarnotta's awful death on TV. There are rumors he was murdered. Is it true?"

"It seems to be," said Montalbano.

"Then it's my duty to give you something. Two days ago,

Guarnotta gave me an envelope, saying I should give it to you if he were suddenly to die violently. Here it is. Have a good day."

And he walked out, leaving the inspector and Fazio completely flummoxed. Montalbano then opened a large linen envelope and pulled out a sheet of paper and three VHS cassettes.

The girl's name was Olga Bernova, and she was nineteen years old. I can't tell you any more than this. She came to my place three times. The idea of filming a gang rape culminating in murder in the presence of a few rich, paying spectators was the idea of Milko Stanic, one of the local importers of girls from Eastern Europe, under the protection of the Cuffaros. The idea was to put the copies of the tape on the market without the knowledge of the participants, who in any case are unrecognizable. The key must certainly have fallen out of my pocket during the filming, and Olga must have noticed. She then scooped it up after being left alone and, knowing she was dying, she came to my place to put you on my scent and on the organization's. She succeeded. As for me, they'll surely make me pay for the mistake of the key.

"Feel up to watching them with me?" Montalbano asked Fazio.

Resigned, Fazio threw up his hands.

It took them three hours to watch them all. They were witness to three murders, three human sacrifices. The girls, poor things, would change, but the participants in both the rapes and the murders, who were ten in number, clearly were always the same people, even though they were always hooded and naked.

"I'm gonna go drink a glass of water," said Fazio, looking pale.

"Bring me one, too, would you?" said the inspector.

He didn't feel like getting up. His legs were as though cut out from under him, and there was a weight pressing down on his chest. The tapes had confirmed his suspicions.

But this gave him no sense of satisfaction. On the contrary. He drank down his water as though dying of thirst.

"I wonder why we never found the bodies of the other two?" Fazio asked himself.

"Maybe they dissolved them in acid," said Montalbano. Then he added: "You know, I recognized one of those hooded men. The short, fat guy with the habit of bringing the thumb and index finger of his left hand together in a circle every five minutes or so."

"Who wouldn't recognize that guy?" Fazio retorted. "He does it even when he appears on TV to talk about Christian values and the sanctity of the family."

"If we tried," said Montalbano, "we could identify another three or four right now. One of them limps and is missing the little finger on his left hand . . ."

"The president of the chamber of commerce, the former undersecretary," Fazio said gloomily.

". . . another guy's got a tattoo of an anchor on his right shoulder; a third's got scars from a recent operation on his chest . . ."

"One is the president of the Nautical Club; the other is the cultural councilor of the provincial government. I saw them once in bathing suits," said Fazio in an almost plaintive tone.

Gaetano Mistretta, the public prosecutor, turned as red as a child's ball when he heard the identifications. Wiping the sweat from his brow, he said:

"Leave the cassettes here with me and don't say anything about them to anybody. You will no longer be involved in the investigation. Nor will Inspector Gianquinto. Our homicide unit will take charge. That's an order, and that's final."

Montalbano got up and left without a word.

He did not protest. It would have been pointless. He knew how it would have ended up.

Following standard procedure, Prosecutor Gaetano Mistretta catalogued the note and the videocassettes and put them in a file, to which he affixed the label, in accordance with standard procedure (and with the dictates of caution), "The State vs. Persons Unknown."

Before leaving the office after the day's work, Prosecutor Gaetano Mistretta took the file, "The State vs. Persons Unknown," and, following standard procedure, put it in a drawer of his desk, which he then locked with a key.

And, once again in accordance with standard procedure, that night, two burglars entered Prosecutor Gaetano Mistretta's office and, knowing exactly what they were looking for, made off with that file and nothing else.

Knowing, however, what was going to happen in accordance with standard procedure, Inspector Salvo Montalbano had also followed standard procedure. That is, before turning Guarnotta's letter and the three cassettes over to the DA, he'd had Catarella make him a copy of the letter as well as copies of the three tapes.

And he hid them well, in hopes of better days to come.

THE APRICOT

1

Livia was supposed to be landing at Punta Raisi airport on the eight-thirty p.m. flight, but Montalbano wasn't able to embrace her until nine-thirty, because the plane came in an hour late. Since it was Saturday and he had nothing to do at the office, he'd decided to drive to Palermo to pick her up.

It was a soft, late September evening, calm and inviting, the kind that makes you want to sleep outside, under the stars.

"Do you want to go straight to Vigàta?"

He had no idea how much he would regret having asked her this careless question.

"Well, I think we won't get back before eleven, and it'll be too late to go and eat at Calogero's. Don't you have anything in the house?"

"No."

"So what should we do?"

"I don't know. I wouldn't mind driving around a little."

"Do you want to go into Palermo?"

"Are you kidding! I want to breathe the air of the sea . . . Listen, why don't we drive down the coastal road? It's a longer route, but it's not as if anyone's waiting for us. And anyway . . ."

"Anyway?"

"If we felt like it, we could just check into the first hotel we come across and spend the night there."

They hadn't been driving for half an hour when Livia said:

"Man, am I ever getting hungry!"

"Let's wait until we get to where I have in mind to go."

Fifteen minutes later they were sitting down at a table in a trattoria almost at the water's edge. Montalbano knew from personal experience that they served the freshest fish there.

Livia might be hungry, but the inspector was a starving wolf.

They took things slow and easy, so much so that by the time they'd finished drinking their second glasses of digestive limoncello, they both felt the need to take a long walk along the wet sand.

A full moon hovered like a hot-air balloon in the sky above.

When they got back in the car it was after midnight.

"Drive really slowly."

"Why?"

"Just because."

Having given her exhaustive explanation, Livia leaned her head back, closed her eyes, and went right to sleep.

Ten minutes later Montalbano began to wonder whether sleep might not be contagious. His eyelids were drooping dangerously. Or had he perhaps had a little too much of that white wine?

Whatever the case, it's never a good idea to keep driving

when sleepiness comes over you. So, seeing an open area beside the road, he pulled over, turned off the engine, got com-
fortable in his seat, and closed his eyes.

I'll wake myself up in half an hour, he thought.

Half an hour, right. When he opened his eyes again he realized it was four o'clock in the morning! The nap had done
him good, however. He felt lucid and rested.

He started up the car. Livia woke up at once.

"Hey, what time is it?"

"Four."

"Why aren't we home yet?"

"I fell asleep, too."

"Where are we?"

"In about half an hour we'll be at the salt ponds."

"As soon as you see them, pull over."

When they got there, they saw little or nothing of the salt
ponds, despite the moonlight. Livia stepped out of the car and
looked around in disappointment. Then she said:

"Take me up there."

"To Erice?"

"Yes. I want to see the sun rise over the salt ponds."

He didn't feel up to refusing. And so they watched the
sun rise over the salt ponds. And it was worth it, even though,
by this point, the inspector, strangely enough, really wanted
to lie down in a bed.

They set off again.

"When we get to Montallegro, turn off the main road
and take the one that runs along the shore."

Montalbano didn't breathe a word. The coastal road in this area was poorly maintained and chunks of the asphalt surface were missing in spots. There were also rises and dips, and occasional landslides, but the view was superb.

They drove past Montereale and entered the municipal territory of Vigàta, which would soon appear almost directly beneath them, once past the curve they were taking at that very moment, which was known as the "Calizzi bend."

As soon as he'd rounded the bend, however, the inspector braked.

"What's wrong?" asked Livia.

"I don't know," said Montalbano.

"Are you going to take another nap right here?" Livia asked sarcastically.

Montalbano didn't reply. He put the car in reverse and slowly backed up. He could do whatever he liked, because there were never any cars on that road. He stopped to look at the guardrail.

It had been broken some time before by a truck that ended up a hundred feet below on the beach, and no one had repaired it since then.

"What's wrong?" Livia asked again.

"The fact is that I passed this way yesterday afternoon, and the guardrail was not . . ."

"Was not what?" Livia pressed him, impatiently.

"It wasn't hanging over the void like that. It looks as though another car has crashed against it."

"So let's go and have a look, no?"

They got out of the car, looked out over the edge of the road and onto the beach below.

There they saw a car completely upside down. One of the wheels was still turning ever so slowly and then stopped, right before their eyes.

"Oh, my God!" said Livia.

"You stay here," said Montalbano. "I'm going down to have a look. If any cars pass, stop them. I'm going to need some help."

———

He very nearly broke his neck twice. Had he looked, he probably could have found a little footpath leading to the beach, but he hadn't wanted to waste any time. When he reached the sand, he was just four steps away from the car. By now the morning light was bright and he could see well.

He flopped to the ground on his stomach. The driver's-side window was shattered and half-gone. There was a woman inside, but he couldn't see her face. He could tell her sex from her long, bloodied blond hair. Pushing her hair aside, he was able to put his hand under her throat . . . There was no doubt . . . No heartbeat. Something hard rolled out next to his hand. It was an apple. He put it in his pocket. He looked long and hard through what remained of the other windows until he was absolutely certain there were no other bodies in the car.

He got back on his feet and looked up. Livia was above him, watching him from the edge of the road. He cupped his hands around his mouth.

"Have any other cars passed?" he asked.

"No."

"Then get in the car and drive until you find a phone,

211

then call my office and tell them there's a dead body at the Calizzi bend. Then come back."

He took the apple out of his pocket and looked at it. The woman had probably brought it along to eat while driving. He tossed it back into the car, went down to the water's edge, fired up a cigarette, and walked along the beach, smoking.

He felt a little disoriented. Maybe from the strange night he'd just had. Or maybe there was something else . . .

Yes, but what? That was the question.

Fazio and Gallo arrived about forty-five minutes later. Montalbano told Livia to go on ahead to Marinella in his car. He'd have the others take him home in the squad car. The firemen who arrived on the scene quickly concluded that without the help of a crane they would never be able to turn the car over to pull the body out. It had sunk too far down into the dry sand.

The fire chief looked thoughtfully up at the cliff the car had fallen from.

"Notice anything?" Montalbano asked him.

"The car must have flipped when it crashed into that spur there, as it fell. You see?"

"Yes. And so?"

"This means that the car was not speeding as it took the curve. Actually, I would even say it was going very slowly."

"What makes you—"

"If it had jumped the curve with even a little speed, it would have flown past that spur, which doesn't stick out very far, and would certainly not have flipped over."

"I see. So you think the accident may have occurred when the driver suddenly fell asleep or passed out?"

"I would say so."

It was possible that if he hadn't pulled over and taken that little nap, he might have met the same end as the poor woman who crashed onto the beach.

Dr. Pasquano arrived and completely lost it when he saw the situation.

"What the fuck is the point of calling me if I can't even examine the body?"

Then, when told that it would be another hour, maybe more, before the crane arrived, he told the orderlies to bring the body to the morgue when it was freed, then got back into his car and drove off cursing, and without saying good-bye to anyone.

The crane arrived an hour later and had to maneuver for another hour before finding the right position for lifting the car.

Now the dead woman could finally be pulled out, and Montalbano could get a look at her face. She must have been very pretty, and looked to be in her early twenties.

Seeing that the prosecutor still hadn't deigned to arrive, the inspector had Gallo drive him home.

He found Livia on the beach in a bathing suit.

"I'm going to take a shower, and then I'll join you," he said.

Livia, keeping her eyes closed all the while, mumbled something he didn't understand.

As he was undressing in the bathroom, he looked at his watch. It was already eleven o'clock. He stayed a long time in the shower. Then he put on his bathing suit, came out of the bathroom, and headed for the door.

"Where are you going?"

It was Livia. Who was lying on the bed, laughing.

"Listen, if we get up now and hurry, we can still make it to Calogero's."

"Mmmm . . ."

"Is that a yes mmmm or a no mmmm?"

"Mmmm."

She probably meant no, Montalbano decided.

And he fell asleep without realizing.

He was in his car alone and driving. He'd been going for hours and hours, on his way back to Marinella from Paris, where he'd gone to do something he couldn't remember. But when he reached the Italian border, the French customs agent said he had to go the long way, through Switzerland.

"Why?"

"It's a state secret. And you have to reach the Swiss border within three hours, otherwise you won't be able to cross there, either."

So he'd driven off and come to a stop in front of a fruit-and-vegetable stand and bought three apples and a pear. He couldn't stop to eat; that would waste too much time. When he reached the Swiss-Italian border, the Swiss customs agents started kicking up a row when they saw, in the passenger's seat, the pear he hadn't eaten beside the only remaining apple.

"Get out of the car. You are under arrest."

"But what for?"

"You tried to illegally export a pear."

"What about the apple?"

"That's all right. Apples are not under restriction."

Had everyone gone insane? He got out of the car and grabbed the customs agent by the shoulders, who responded with a punch. Montalbano then dealt him a swift kick, yelling desperately.

He was woken up by his own yells and lay there panting and sweaty. He looked at his watch: a little after seven.

Livia was asleep. He shook her.

"Come on, wake up. I don't feel like skipping dinner."

2

The moment he walked into headquarters, Catarella snapped to attention and assailed him.

"Ahh, Chief, Chief! Ahh, Chief! Hizzoner the C'mishner jess called jess now not a minnit ago!"

"What did he want?"

"I dunno, 'e dun't truss me to take a messitch."

"But did he tell you anything?"

"Yessir. 'E said ya gotta call me as soon as ya gets in."

"He wants me to call you?"

"Nossir, Chief, not me insomuch as 'im, nossir. But me meanin' Hizzoner the C'mishner."

Montalbano went into his office and dialed the commissioner's number.

"What is it, sir?"

"Nothing in particular, Montalbano. But is it true that your girlfriend from Genoa is here?"

Was it ever possible to keep anything secret in that town? How the hell did everybody know everything about everyone?

"Yes, Mr. Commissioner."

"And is it true that her surname is Burlando, like mine?"

"Yes."

"Listen, why don't the two of you come to dinner at our place this evening? It was my wife's idea. Otherwise I wouldn't have bothered you."

Could he possibly back out? He couldn't.

"We'd be delighted to come. Thank you. See you this evening."

The commissioner was a fine gentleman whom the inspector liked, and his wife was someone who knew what to do with a cooker. At any rate Livia wouldn't have any objection.

Fazio then appeared and asked for permission to enter.

"What time did you guys finish up at the Calizzi bend yesterday?"

"Good God, Chief, I don't even want to hear about it! The prosecutor made us wait three hours! And even the Road Police showed up!"

"And wha'd they say?"

"They came to the conclusion that, even though she was going slow, the girl showed no sign of having tried to take the curve, but drove straight off the edge. So it must be a case of suicide or an accident caused by falling asleep at the wheel or some other malaise on the driver's part."

"Tell me something. I saw an apple inside the car. Were there any others?"

"Yessir, there were three apples. She was keeping them in a large paper bag, probably on the passenger's seat."

"Did anyone find the remains of the other apples she'd eaten?"

"No, she probably threw them out the window."

The dream he'd had suggested the next question.

"Were there any pears?"

"Nah. Why do you ask?"

"No reason. Never mind. Do you know what her name was?"

"Of course. Annarosa Testa. She was twenty-three years old and lived alone, here in Vigàta, at Via Mistretta, number forty-eight."

"Why alone?"

"Her father and mother live in Milan. They moved there two years ago. But I'm told the girl didn't spend much time at home, hardly any at all. She traveled a lot."

"Who traveled a lot?" asked Mimì Augello, walking in.

"Some girl who died yesterday morning in a car accident," the inspector replied.

"Ah," said Mimì. "Poor Annarosa! I knew her!"

As if he wouldn't have known her! How could you go wrong? Mimì had exclusive rights to all the pretty girls not only in Vigàta, but the entire province.

"Then tell me a little about her."

"But they said on TV that it was an accident! Why would you want to know—"

"Think you can muster the effort to tell me what she did for a living?"

"Salvo, she did what so many other girls do these

days! One day she modeled, another day, when possible, she worked in advertising, or else served as an usherette at some convention . . . Stuff like that."

"Did she have a boyfriend?"

"For about a year, maybe a little longer, she was with Giuliano Toccaceli, the son of Fofò Toccaceli, the clothing wholesaler. But they'd broken up recently because he was very jealous, and she used to allow herself an occasional, well, 'remunerative escapade.' More than that, I can't tell you."

They then started discussing a pair of burglaries in two different apartments that appeared to be the work of the same hand.

Livia came by to pick him up in the car she'd rented, and they went to eat at Calogero's.

When the inspector told her about the dinner invitation at the commissioner's house, she twisted up her mouth and protested.

"But I didn't bring anything to wear!"

"What are you thinking? They're very informal people. You'll see, you'll fit right in."

After lunch, she dropped him back off at the station and went to the Scala dei Turchi for a solitary swim.

At around five o'clock, Annarosa all of a sudden came charging back into his thoughts. The uneasiness he'd felt when looking at the overturned car on the beach overcame him again, this time more clearly and insistently. He had to do something to calm himself down. The only solution was to find out more.

He picked up the receiver and dialed a number.

"Inspector Montalbano here. Is Dr. Pasquano in?"

"Yes. Do you want me . . ."

It was probably best to talk to him in person.

"No, that's okay. Do you know whether he'll be in his office much longer?"

"Definitely until seven. If he's not called out of the office, that is."

He got in his car, drove off, pulled up in front of the Caffè Castiglione, bought a tray of six cannoli, and headed off again. Less than half an hour later he was parking in front of the Institute of Forensic Science.

"The doctor's in his office," said the assistant.

Montalbano knocked.

"Come in!"

He opened the door and went in. Pasquano, who was sitting at his desk, writing, looked up and cursed.

"What's the ballbusting about this time?"

"No ballbusting, Doctor. I took the liberty of bringing you six perfectly fresh cannoli."

He set the packet down on the desk. Pasquano, who had a severe sweet tooth, opened it, took out a cannolo, and started eating it.

"Not bad. And what, may I ask, is the price of this corruption?" he asked with his mouth full.

"I want to know why the girl who drove off the cliff didn't take the curve but went straight."

"Ah."

He gestured to Montalbano to sit down. Before answering, he inhaled another cannolo.

"Have you ever found yourself with a piece of meat or

bread stuck in your throat that won't go down and won't come up?"

"Yes, that happened to me once. A chunk of meat too big and insufficiently chewed."

"Do you remember how it felt?"

"It felt like I was choking to death. I couldn't breathe. I flew into a panic."

"You're describing exactly what happened to that poor girl."

"A piece of apple got stuck in her throat and she lost control of herself and her car?"

"That's exactly right. But why did you mention an apple?"

"Because there were still three apples in the car."

"Yes, but what stuck in her throat was the pit of a large apricot."

"But there weren't any apricots in the car!"

"So what? Apparently she'd eaten them all, and the last one was fatal."

There was only one cannolo left in the tray. Pasquano grabbed it.

"Want half?"

Montalbano declined magnanimously.

As soon as he got back to the station, he summoned Fazio.

"Listen, I was wondering: Are you sure there weren't also any apricot pits in Annarosa's car?"

Fazio gave him a puzzled look.

"Chief, first you come out with the question about the pear, and now the apricots. What are you looking for?"

"I don't know. But I feel restless."

"I already told you, Chief. All we found in that car was three apples."

Montalbano told him what Pasquano had said. And Fazio came to the same conclusion as the doctor.

"She probably ate them all, and the last one, poor thing . . ."

The dinner was a real family affair.

The commissioner and Livia spent a good hour trying to figure out whether or not they were related, since they shared the last name of Burlando; but, try as they might, they were unable to find any relation whatsoever, however distant.

Signora Burlando cooked like a goddess, and Montalbano had a feast.

Then the conversation turned to the accident at the Calizzi bend, and Montalbano mentioned the conclusion that Dr. Pasquano had come to.

"Strange," the commissioner commented.

Everyone, Montalbano included, looked at him questioningly.

"It's strange," the commissioner went on, taking an apricot from the fruit bowl in the middle of the table, "because today's apricots are not what they used to be."

"I don't understand," said the inspector.

"Apricots used to be much smaller, softer, and a whole lot tastier. You could put one in your mouth and then spit out the pit. Now take a look at the apricot I'm holding. It's big and hard. You could never put the whole thing in your mouth. You have to split it in two with your fingers, like this, eat one half, then remove the pit wedged in the other half, and then eat that one, too. If you're driving, you have no choice but to take your hands off the wheel."

"Come to think of it," Montalbano cut in, "Dr. Pasquano told me the apricot pit was rather large."

"You see? Just as I was saying. At any rate, the girl didn't choke to death, did she?"

"No, Dr. Pasquano maintains that she died when she broke her neck in the crash. And she had another fatal wound in her chest, from the steering wheel. The apricot pit was only the reason why she lost control of the car."

"Couldn't you please talk about something else?" Signora Burlando intervened. "It's not very pleasant hearing about this."

When they got to their car to go home to Marinella, Montalbano asked Livia if she could drive.

"No problem."

They set off. A few minutes later, the inspector took an apricot out of his pocket.

"Where'd you get that?"

"I stole it, right before getting up from the table."

"Are you crazy? What if they saw you?"

"They didn't see anything, don't worry. Would you do me a favor?"

"One is always supposed to say yes to the insane."

"Take it and eat it while still driving."

Livia slowed down. Then, steadying the wheel with her forearms, she split the apricot in two, using both hands, and then brought the first half to her mouth and ate it.

"That wasn't easy to chew, you know. If it was up to me, I would rather have eaten it in two bites."

"Now try to put the other half in your mouth, with the pit, as if you'd forgotten to remove it."

Livia tried, but a second later spat everything out.

"You can't swallow it that way. You'd have to swallow it whole, because with the pit in there, it's impossible to chew. You'll break your teeth. Nobody could be so distracted as to do something like that. You have no choice but to take the pit out first."

So why hadn't Annarosa taken it out?

3

When he got up the following morning to go into the bathroom, to avoid waking Livia, who was in a cataleptic state, he tried not to make any noise at all and had a stupid accident, of the kind that throw you into a rage more for their idiocy than for any harm done.

Still sleepy as he was, since the coffee was percolating just then and he hadn't yet been able to drink any, he picked up his toothbrush, only to let it slip out of his hand and fall to the floor at his feet.

He instinctively bent straight down, promptly crashing his nose against the edge of the sink.

Cursing the saints through clenched teeth, he recovered the toothbrush, and as he was putting it under the spout to rinse it off, he realized his hand was covered in blood.

And where did that come from?

Looking in the mirror, he saw that it was pouring out of his nose from the blow.

He raced into the kitchen, tilting his head back, opened the freezer, took out an ice cube, placed it against the bridge of his nose, and sat down. After a short while the bleeding stopped, and he cleaned his hands and face in the kitchen, drank down a mug of espresso, and went back into the bathroom.

But as he was taking his shower he felt uneasy. There was something that didn't add up in the connection between his grabbing the toothbrush and then noticing the blood on his hand.

But it was all perfectly logical, wasn't it? Why get all contorted over something so simple?

You crouch down, pick up the toothbrush, bring it towards yourself, and at that moment a drop of blood falls from your nose and onto the hand holding the toothbrush.

What's so strange about that, Montalbà? Nothing?

Then stop racking your brains over it.

"Livia, I'm leaving, to go to work."

"Mmmm."

"We'll talk later."

"Mmmm."

He got in his car, drove down the dirt path that led to the main road, and then had to come to a halt. In front of him was a wall of automobiles and trucks wedged so tightly bumper to bumper that there was no way for him to slip in. The only hope was to try the "gangster method," which consisted of advancing one centimeter at a time until the front of his car gradually blocked the headlight of the next car in line in such a way that it could no longer go forward. In this fashion, he could work his way in.

It took him about ten minutes to complete the maneuver, after which he was in line with the rest. In front of him was a rickety old jalopy with a flapping canvas for a roof, which surely ran on wine instead of gasoline, since it was constantly swerving to either side like a drunkard.

Behind him was a sparkling new BMW, looking all arrogant and aggressive, making clear to all concerned its great itch to pass Montalbano and the jalopy.

Then at one point the great car's itchy driver's patience ran out, and, wildly honking his horn, he began to accelerate. With a swerve worthy of a Grand Prix contestant, Montalbano cleared the path for him.

For a second the BMW pulled up beside him, then accelerated again and passed him, and at that exact moment the drunken jalopy decided to veer to the left.

The collision was unavoidable, as the BMW didn't have time to brake.

Hit from behind on the left side, the jalopy swerved right, flew into the air, over the road, and came down nose-first in a shallow ditch, its two rear wheels spinning in the air.

Having immediately slammed on his brakes, Montalbano got out of the car and ran to help out the driver of the jalopy. The man driving the BMW also got out and was running up to them. Everyone else had stopped to look on.

Meanwhile, however, the driver of the jalopy had crawled out of his vehicle and stood up with flames shooting out of his eyes. He appeared uninjured.

"Who hit me?" he asked.

"I did," replied the driver of the BMW.

And he was unable to say any more, as the driver of the jalopy was all over him. The two began to exchange punches and kicks.

"Come on, knock it off!" said Montalbano, trying to separate the two.

Then, all at once, he froze, mouth agape.

He was staring at one of the jalopy's wheels, which was still turning, more and more slowly.

It was still turning!

Then it stopped.

It had stopped!

"Ahhh!"

The yell that escaped the inspector's lips was so wild and powerful that the two men scuffling stopped, speechless, and looked at him.

The inspector then seemed to go insane.

He raced back to his car, threw it into reverse, crashing against the other vehicles as if driving a bumper car at the amusement park, somehow managed to maneuver his way into the other lane, and five minutes later was opening the door to his house.

He ran into the bedroom. Livia was still asleep.

"Livia!"

He'd wanted to say it softly, but the voice that came out was somewhere between a wolf's howl and a Tarzan yell.

Livia woke up with a start.

And before her eyes she saw a wild-eyed, disheveled Montalbano with blood trickling from his lower lip, a consequence of his attempt to separate the two brawling men.

And she got scared to death.

"Oh, my God, what happened to you?"

Montalbano raised one hand and, in a Grand Inquisitor–like gesture, pointed his index finger at her.

"Was it spinning or not?"

Upon hearing the question, Livia's fear turned into pure terror.

She shot to her feet right in bed and recoiled against the wall.

"Calm down, Salvo, I beg you!"

"But was it spinning?"

"Was what spinning?"

"The wheel."

"What wheel?"

Realizing that he was getting nowhere this way, Montalbano sat down at the foot of the bed and tried to calm down.

"Why are you standing?"

"I dunno," Livia said in a phony tone of unconcern.

"Then lie back down."

Livia obeyed without a word. Salvo ran his hands over his face.

"I'm sorry I woke you up like that, but there was . . ."

"It's okay."

"I just wanted to ask you something."

"Go ahead, please," Livia said eagerly.

Seeing that he was calming down, she thought it was best to give him some rope.

"The other morning, at the bend, when we looked out over the edge to see what had happened, and we saw that overturned car on the beach below us, do you remember . . . ?"

"Of course I remember."

"Okay. Wasn't one of the car's wheels still turning?"

"Yes. Very slowly. And it stopped as we were watching."

Without saying a word, Montalbano hugged her and kissed her. Then he said:

"Go back to sleep. I'm going to the office."

"Who could go back to sleep after that? But can I get an explanation later?"

"Sure."

He noticed immediately that the great traffic jam had ended. Without bothering to stop at the office, he headed straight for Montelusa and a short while later pulled up outside the institute.

"Dr. Pasquano in?"

"Not yet. But he should be here at any moment."

He went out into the parking lot to smoke a cigarette. Then he saw Pasquano's car pull in. He ran up to it and opened the door.

"While you're at it," said the doctor, "why don't you give me a little shoe shine as well?"

Poker-faced, the inspector took a handkerchief out of his pocket and started to kneel down.

"So it's something really big," said the doctor.

"Huge."

"Then please hurry, I've got a dead body waiting for me."

"Are you aware that it was I who discovered the car that plunged off the Calizzi bend?"

"No, I didn't know. My most heartfelt compliments. So what?"

"The accident had happened just moments before."

"Moments before, my ass. How can you say that?"

"One of the wheels was still turning."

"Apparently you hadn't entirely slept off your drunken stupor of the night before."

"The person who was with me also saw the wheel turning."

"What time was it?"

"About six in the morning."

"Was there wind?"

"No. Tell me something. In your opinion, how much earlier had the accident happened, which I thought occurred right before six o'clock?"

"At least six hours before you discovered it. The girl died around midnight."

"And how will you react if I venture a hypothesis?"

"It depends. Either with a kick to your grimaldis or an invitation to continue the discussion in my office."

"What if the accident was used to cover up a murder?"

Dr. Pasquano thought about this for a moment.

"Let's go into my office."

"But what was it that aroused your suspicion?" was the first thing Pasquano asked as soon as they sat down.

"Something I unconsciously realized at once, but didn't immediately understand. When I went to check whether the girl might be still alive, I pushed aside her bloodied hair, then picked up an apple that had rolled near her head and . . . I didn't get any blood on my hand."

"Because it had already clotted," said Pasquano.

"Right. Except that I didn't think of that. Then I witnessed, this morning, another car accident, I saw another car wheel spinning in the air, and I tied it all together."

"So how do you think the whole thing went?" Pasquano asked.

And Montalbano started talking.

An hour later he was in his Vigàta office with Fazio and Augello.

". . . so they have a violent altercation, the man grabs her and puts her in a headlock, she tries to struggle free, kicking and flailing, and before he knows it, the man finds her dead in his arms, having broken her neck. After an initial moment of panic, the man tries to think of a way to get rid of the body. And while he's thinking, two or three hours pass without him even noticing. The more time goes by, the more the guy frets, because he hasn't the slightest idea what he should do. So, since the squabble started right after they'd finished eating, the guy probably sits down at the table and has a glass of wine. And at that moment, it becomes perfectly clear what he has to do. He takes a big apricot, breaks it in two, takes out the pit, and, with this in his hand, bends over the girl's body and puts the pit in her mouth, pushing it into her throat with his fingers, where the pit then gets stuck. Then he hoists the corpse onto his shoulders, sits it down in the car, tightening the seat belt over it as far as it will go, gets into the driver's seat, goes to the Calizzi bend, stops the car right at the edge of the cliff with the motor running, gets out, moves the corpse into the driver's seat, puts the seat belt back on it, releases the break, and gets out and starts pushing. The car lurches, hits the guardrail, and plummets below. The man probably then went and hid on the other side of the road, where the grass is high. He may even have still been there when Livia and I showed up. So, what do you guys think?"

"It's a nice little novel you've written there. To me it makes a whole lot of sense. But will the prosecutor like it?"

"What about you, Fazio?"

"I agree with Inspector Augello. What's our evidence? A spinning tire. A simple gust of wind could—"

"Enough of this shit! There wasn't any wind!"

"The car could have shifted in the sand . . ."

"That's more likely. So what do we do now?"

"Let's try to find out more about the girl," Augello suggested.

They all agreed on this.

4

As he was about to go out to Calogero's, Livia called to tell him she would rather stay home, and at that moment he had an idea. Where had Fazio said the girl lived? Ah, yes. Via Mistretta, 48.

He drove there. Right beside the front door to the building was a greengrocer's shop.

He parked, got out, and went in. The owner of the shop was a fat, fiftyish woman with a mustache and a likable manner.

"What can I get for you?"

"I'm a police inspector."

"Do you want to arrest me?" the woman said, laughing.

"I just want to ask you for some information. Did Annarosa, the poor girl who died, buy her fruit here from you?"

The woman's expression changed completely.

"The poor thing! What a terrible end! Yessir, she always came and bought her groceries here. Then she would get in her car and eat fruit as she drove."

"What kinds of fruit did she like?"

"She liked apples best of all. But also pears, cherries, medlars . . . depending on the season."

"How about apricots?"

"No, no apricots. She couldn't even stand to touch them. She was allergic to them."

A beautiful sun was shining, but for Montalbano it immediately became a thousand times brighter.

Even Calogero was a little shocked at the amount of food the inspector managed to cram into his stomach.

"What are you doing, Inspector, loading up in case of famine?"

Montalbano had no choice but to take a long walk along the jetty, otherwise he risked falling asleep the moment he returned to his office.

He found Augello at the station, but not Fazio.

"Feel like going to see the prosecutor, Mimì?"

"But we said we'd—"

"There's a new development."

And he told him, adding:

"The grocer lady is willing to testify that Annarosa was allergic to apricots. Apparently her killer didn't know that."

"Therefore they hadn't known each other for very long."

"That's quite likely. Oh, and Mimì, I want you to get everything back: her house keys, purse, everything."

Just as Augello was going out, Fazio came in. Montalbano also told him about the girl's allergy. And Fazio said the same thing as Mimì.

"That means the killer hadn't known Annarosa for very long."

"Don't you, too, get started on that," Montalbano reacted.

"Get started on what?"

"Look, you can't be sure about that. Maybe the killer had been with her for a good while but they'd never eaten together or talked about fruit. Or else . . ."

"Or else . . ."

"Nothing. Just an idea I had. Too complicated to explain. Never mind."

Augello got back around six. The prosecutor had opened a case file for murder by persons unknown. The investigation could now get under way. Mimì had also brought back the keys and the large handbag. Inside the latter, aside from a wallet with IDs and five hundred lire, and the usual feminine things, including a little beauty kit, there was also a pair of clean panties and bra inside a plastic bag.

"Let's go and have a look at the girl's home," said Montalbano.

"Want to bet we'll find her parents there?" said Augello.

"No, we won't," Fazio interjected, being always the best informed of the three. "The girl's mother, as soon as she heard the news, had a cardiac episode and was hospitalized, and her husband doesn't want to leave her side."

Annarosa's apartment was small and in perfect order. The armoire in the bedroom was full of very fine clothes and fancy underwear. In the little hallway was a second, tiny armoire. In the large, well-lit bathroom was a white chest stuffed full of creams, perfumes, little jars, and tubes. All the walls in the apartment were plastered with photos of her: in a bathing suit, in a long dress, in jeans, in skirt and blouse, as well as close-ups of her beautiful face. In one corner of the little living room was a tiny desk with a telephone and a small answering machine beside it.

Montalbano pressed the "listen" button, and three messages began playing. The first was from Annarosa's mother, who asked her to call back. The second was from a Milanese girlfriend who mentioned a photo shoot. The third was a male voice that said, "This is Giuliano," and he, too, wanted Annarosa to call him back as soon as she returned. When the tape finished, a canned voice said these messages were left on the afternoon of the previous Friday. In a small closet they found a complete set of elegant suitcases, and another medium-sized one of a different color.

"If you ask me," said Augello, "the girl was not returning from a trip. And in fact we didn't find any baggage in her car. She'd only brought what she needed to spend the night out."

"Okay, now we'll ask for confirmation," said Montalbano.

When they were out on the street, the inspector went straight into the greengrocer's shop.

"I'm sorry, Signora, but do you remember the last time Annarosa bought some fruit from you?"

"Of course I remember. She bought five apples. It was probably around eight o'clock last Saturday evening, 'cause I was already closing up shop."

"Did she say anything to you?"

"She said: 'I'll see you Monday.' Then she got in her car and left."

"How was she dressed?"

"In jeans and a blouse, and wearing the usual coral necklace, which she was really fond of."

Montalbano and Fazio exchanged a meaningful glance. No trace of that necklace had been found in the overturned car.

They held a brief meeting at the station. The only way to find out more about Annarosa was to talk to Giuliano Toccaceli, her ex-boyfriend, the one who'd left a message. Fazio went to call him, and they arranged for him to come to the office at nine the following morning.

Montalbano grabbed his agenda and went home, where he found Livia sitting on the veranda, watching the sea.

"What are you doing?"

"Training."

"For what?"

"For getting used to your absence."

He noticed that Duilio, a fisherman, was pulling his boat to shore.

"Excuse me just a minute."

Montalbano went down onto the beach, exchanged a few words with Duilio, and came back to the veranda.

"Excuse me just a minute."

Livia looked at him in shock and was even more shocked when she heard the sound of Salvo getting back in his car and driving away.

Half an hour later he returned with a large plastic bag in his hand. In it, Livia got a glimpse of some wrapped-up panini and two bottles of wine.

"Let's go."

He took her by the hand and led her to Duilio's boat.

"Take off your sandals and help me get the boat in the water."

They ate and drank on the open sea, and spent three enchanted hours in the boat. They even made love in it. Then, upon returning, Livia went to bed, and Montalbano joined her.

Before receiving Toccaceli, Montalbano pointed out to Fazio and Augello that if the girl bought fruit at eight in the evening and was killed just after midnight, after having eaten, she could not have gone very far from Vigàta. Then he had Giuliano come in.

He was an elegant man of about forty with refined manners, the classic tall, dark, and handsome type. He wasn't the least bit nervous.

"Signor Toccaceli, as you were told over the phone, this is about the tragic accident that killed Annarosa Testa, who it turns out had been your girlfriend."

"Yes, we were together until late May. But what is there to discuss? Isn't the whole thing pretty clear, unfortunately?"

"The accident, yes, but what caused the accident is not clear. It could have been a sudden malaise that came over her as she was driving back to Vigàta around midnight, shortly after she'd finished dinner. Since you knew her well, we'd like to know whether, for example, she drank too much, or took drugs . . ."

"Are you kidding?" Toccaceli snapped. "She was a very wholesome girl! I'm sorry, but didn't the autopsy—"

"It hasn't been performed yet," Montalbano lied.

"Ah, okay. The only thing she had a weakness for was fruit. God, did she ever eat a lot of it! Except for apricots, that is. She was allergic to them."

"Oh, really?" said Montalbano, showing interest.

"Yes, she only needed to take one in her hand for her skin to break out in a rash and for her to start sneezing—"

"Listen," the inspector said, interrupting him. "After the two of you broke up, did you ever try to see Annarosa again?"

Toccaceli became a little awkward.

"I have to confess that . . . just last Friday I tried to call her. I wanted to see her again. I've never been able to forget her. I wanted her to come to the little house I have by the sea, near Montereale . . . But she adamantly refused."

"Do you know who she was seeing lately?"

"I've heard a few rumors . . . but I wouldn't in any way want to . . . Well, she had a favorite photographer of hers, named Giovagnoli, Marcello Giovagnoli, and apparently over the last few months the two of them—"

Montalbano stood up and held out his hand.

"Thank you so much, and I apologize for having disturbed you. You've been extremely helpful."

Fazio saw the man out and immediately returned.

"So, what was your impression?" the inspector asked his two assistants.

"To me he seemed sincere," said Mimì.

"To me, too," said Fazio.

"To me he smells from a mile away," said Montalbano.

The other two gave a start.

"I'd bet the family jewels that he's the killer," the inspector continued. "He's one very clever son of a bitch. The minute he was told that an autopsy hadn't been done yet he came

237

out with the business about her allergy. And what had we been thinking? That the killer didn't know that Annarosa was allergic to apricots. Therefore, since he himself knew, he couldn't possibly be the killer. Secondly: It's possible that Annarosa hadn't erased his phone message because she wanted us to know. Thirdly: He told us—before we could find out on our own—that he has a little house at Montereale, in other words, not far from the Calizzi bend. How much do you want to bet that this photographer Giovagnoli also has a house near the Calizzi bend?"

"So what's the plan?" asked Fazio, ignoring the challenge of the bet.

"You find out exactly where Toccaceli's house is and let me know."

"If he's as clever as you say, he'll be hard to trap," said Augello.

"Mimì, sometimes these smarty-pants types get screwed by chance."

Montalbano, however, was also of the opinion that chance sometimes needed a little help. And so, after midnight, and after giving Livia an excuse about having some late work to do, he left home and headed for Montereale. Fazio had told him that Toccaceli's little house was green and on the beach, just below Punta Rosa. He had no trouble finding it. It was in a secluded spot. It took him about fifteen minutes to un-lock the door using the various skeleton keys he'd brought with him. He focused all his attention on the dining room, where he thought the quarrel had taken place. It was clean and in perfect order. Toccaceli had surely gone over the whole place with a fine-tooth comb. Montalbano put on his gloves and started looking for something, without knowing what. An hour and a half later he still hadn't found anything, and so he decided to move the furniture and have a look behind the different pieces.

In this way, in a spot hidden behind one of the two rear feet of the hutch, he saw, almost directly against the wall, a tiny piece of red coral, which he picked up and examined. There was no doubt about it. It had been part of a necklace. Apparently the necklace was broken during a struggle, and Toccaceli had collected the pieces and thrown them away who knows where. But as chance would have it, he hadn't seen that minuscule piece.

He put it back in place, arranged the furniture, went out, locked the door again, and returned home.

The following morning he went to see the commissioner and confessed to having conducted an unauthorized search. Burlando flew off the handle, and couldn't even refrain himself from cuffing his subordinate upside the head, but then he did everything in his power to get the prosecutor to authorize a search.

Toccaceli was arrested.

He confessed he killed Annarosa because, after persuading her to spend the weekend with him, swearing he wouldn't lay a hand on her, he'd lost his head after dinner, she'd refused, and . . .

THE HONEST THIEF

1

As Fazio had gone to Palermo to accompany his father for a medical checkup and would be away for a few days, Montalbano summoned Augello when a certain Signor Donato Butera came into the station at nine o'clock one morning to report a burglary of his home.

But it was immediately clear to both Montalbano and Augello that if they were going to deal with Butera they would have to be as patient as saints.

Butera was a well-dressed man of sixty who, upon sitting down, removed his glasses, cleaned them with a handkerchief, adjusted his tie and the crease in his trousers, cleared his throat, pulled his shirt cuffs out from the sleeves of his jacket, adjusted his buttocks on the chair as best he could, and finally made up his mind to speak.

"You must know, Mr. Inspector, that since I'm a widow and have been living alone ever since my only son, Jacono, went to work at a good job in Germany and even got married there, every evening when I come home, I prepare myself a little something to eat. After eating, I sit down in front of the TV with a flask of wine and watch a movie. And then, when I start to feel sleepy, I get up and go to bed."

He took off his glasses and started cleaning them again.

Montalbano and Augello looked at each other in dismay. He sure took his time, this Signor Butera. Then the inspector, feeling a little impatient, said:

"Signor Butera, I'm sorry, but you still haven't told us your reason for coming here . . ."

"Just be patient for a minute, and I'll get to that. But first I have to tell you that before falling asleep, while I'm lying there with my eyes half-closed, I sometimes see characters from the movie walking around the room."

"You see scenes from the film?" Montalbano asked.

"Not scenes, but characters. Like they were there in the flesh."

At this point Augello wanted more details.

"When you're watching the film, do you drink the whole flask of wine?"

"Oh, yes. And, as I was about to say, that was why last night I didn't worry about the man in the beret who was walking around in my bedroom."

Montalbano's patience had run out, and he sat there in silence. Augello asked the questions.

"But, so, was the man in the beret a character in the film or not?"

"I thought he was, at least until this morning."

"And what happened this morning?"

"You need to know something first."

"Then tell me."

"You need to know that before going to bed, I always take my wallet out of my trouser pocket and put it on the bedside table."

"Okay, now we know. Then what happened?"

"This morning, when I looked inside my wallet, I realized there was only five hundred lire where last night I had fifteen hundred."

At this point the inspector decided to intervene.

"Let me get this straight. So, you're saying the burglar stole a thousand lire and left you five hundred?"

"That's correct."

"Doesn't that seem strange to you?"

"Of course it does. Logically speaking, he should have taken all the money. But in fact he didn't."

"Are you absolutely sure that there was fifteen hundred lire in your wallet the night before?"

"Absolutely certain. I was given the money just before coming home, and then I checked again before putting my wallet on the nightstand."

"Was anything else stolen?"

"No, sir, nothing."

"Are you sure?"

"Of course! Just think, right next to the wallet was my watch—and it's a good watch, which my wife, rest her soul, gave me as a present for our silver anniversary—and the burglar didn't touch it."

"Did you notice any signs indicating that your front door had been forced?"

"What kind of signs?"

"Did it look like the lock had been tampered with?"

"No, sir."

"What about the windows?"

"They were all shut tight."

"So how do you think he got in?"

"You're asking me? Then what did I come here for? You're the guys who're supposed to find out."

You couldn't say he was wrong.

"All right, Signor Butera, please follow Inspector Augello, who will take a statement from you. Have a good day."

Augello returned fifteen minutes later.

"If you ask me, he was drunk as a skunk and who the hell knows where he lost his thousand lire, if it was ever in his wallet in the first place," said Augello.

"I agree."

They were both wrong. And the first indications of their mistake came when Catarella informed them that a Signora Fodaro was there to see them. Who naturally was not named Fodaro but Todaro: Nunziata Todaro.

"Mr. Inspector, I work nights lookin' after a ninety-year-old woman. I go to her house at nine in the evening after the woman's daughter has already put her to bed, and I spend the whole night there, till seven in the morning. My son Peppi, who isn't married, lives with me. But by the time I come home in the morning he's already gone, 'cause he leaves at six-thirty to go to work."

"Listen, signora . . ."

"I get it, you want me to hurry up. But if I don't explain the whole story to you good, you won't understand a thing."

Montalbano and Augello exchanged glances and resigned themselves.

"All right, go on."

"But this morning he was there."

"Who was there?" asked Augello, momentarily distracted.

"What do you mean, 'who'? My son Peppi was there. He hadn't left for work yet."

"Was he unwell?" Montalbano ventured.

"Nah, he wa'n't no well or unwell, 'e was mad as a hornet!"

"Why?"

"'Cause he cou'n't find his damned thirteen hunnert lire! All's he could find was three hunnert!"

"But where was the money supposed to be?"

"On the kitchen table."

"Did you put it there yourself?"

"I sure did! The night before, just before going out. He'd asked me for some money 'cause he had to pay the installment on a machine he uses in his workshop."

"So you think there was a burglary?"

"I don't think it! There *was* a burglary! A thousand lire disappeared!"

"And did you give your son another thousand lire?"

"Of course! An' it was all the money I had! Now I don't know how I'm gonna make it to the end of the month!"

Very carefully, Montalbano suggested an explanation.

"Isn't it possible your son might have faked a burglary because he—"

Signora Nunziata understood at once.

"Wha'ss goin' through your head? My son is extremely honest! One time, he found a wallet in the street an'—"

"Okay, okay. Was anything else missing?"

"Not a thing."

"Did your son hear any strange noises during the night?"

"The boy's like a corpse when he's asleep."

"Had the lock on the front door been forced?"

"Never!"

"What floor do you live on?"

"The ground floor."

"Were the windows—"

"The windows all have iron bars."

"Do you have any idea how the thief might have got in?"

"It was a woman."

"Who was?" Augello asked again, newly distracted.

"The thief. In my opinion, it was a girl thief."

"Why do you say that?"

"Because I know who it is!"

"And who would that be?"

"That would be 'Ntonietta Sabatino, a big slut who lives on the second floor and who I think does it with Peppi, an' if y'ask me, that sonofabitch of a son of mine gave her the key so she could come and see him when I'm not around, an' so she took advantage and screwed him out of a thousand lire!"

"But, signora, you have no proof whatsoever that—"

"I don't need no proof, I know wha'ss wha', an' iss azackly the way I'm tellin' you, an' you gotta believe me!"

Montalbano couldn't take any more.

"Listen, Mimì, please accompany the lady into your office and take her statement. But be sure the complaint is against an unknown party, I mean it."

———

After taking the woman's statement, Mimì went back into Montalbano's office.

"What do you think?"

"I think we're looking at an absolute novelty in the history of criminology."

"And what would that be?"

"Does it seem normal to you for a burglar always to steal only a thousand lire? What is he, some kind of fixed-rate burglar?"

"What do you think you'll do?"

"Nothing, for the time being. Let's wait for the next burglary and see. A burglar who takes only a thousand lire a pop isn't exactly going to be on easy street. He has no choice but to keep burgling."

Events did not prove him wrong. Three days later, a Monday, a certain Beniamino Dimeli came in to the station at around noon.

He was a well-groomed man of about fifty, impeccably dressed and scented with cologne, quick to bow and flash a toothy smile.

"I'm terribly embarrassed to waste your time with something so silly, but since it's my custom to obey the law, I think it's only right that everyone should obey it."

He smiled. If he was expecting applause from Montalbano or Augello, he was disappointed. But he didn't show it.

"I'm here to report a burglary," he said.

"Of a thousand lire?" Montalbano asked him hopefully.

Dimeli looked at him in shock.

"If it had only been a thousand lire, I would never have—"

"I'm sorry. Please tell us everything."

"I'm from Montelusa, and I still live there. But I also have a small house on the seashore, just past the Scala dei Turchi."

Montalbano gave him a dirty look. So this was the owner of that big, horrendous house recently and clearly illegally built up there with no regard whatsoever for laws, rules, restrictions, and other related impediments.

"I sometimes use it on weekends in the winter. We go—"

"You and your family?" asked Augello.

"No, I'm not married. I go there with three or four friends on Friday evenings, and my friends usually leave at the break of dawn on Monday morning, because they have to go to work. Since I don't have any fixed schedule and have to lock up the house, I always leave later."

"What line of work are you in?" Montalbano asked.

"Me? I . . . have a private income."

"I see. Tell me something. Is it only men who come with you on these weekends?"

"Yes," said Dimeli, smiling. "But I wouldn't want you to get the wrong idea. We're all old friends and now and then we like to amuse ourselves playing a bit of poker far from prying eyes."

"For high stakes?"

"We can afford it."

"So tell us what happened."

"Last night we stopped playing at around four a.m., and my friends decided to leave right then and there. As for me, I locked the doors and windows and, half an hour later, I was already asleep. When I woke up around nine, I realized I'd been robbed."

"What did they steal?"

"I'd left my winnings on the table, after counting them. Exactly one hundred thousand lire. This morning, there was only eighty thousand."

"Are you sure you counted carefully?"

"Quite sure. And I don't understand how the burglar got inside, or why he didn't take it all."

2

"So, naturally you weren't woken up by any strange noises or anything suspicious?"

"No, absolutely not. And I assure you, I'm a very light sleeper, and it doesn't take much to wake me up."

For no apparent reason, Montalbano got it in his head to continue this line of questioning.

"And before?"

"I don't understand?"

"Did you notice anything unusual before going to sleep? You know, something that may seem of no importance to you can be quite crucial to us."

"No, I didn't." He paused ever so briefly, then added: "But . . ."

"But?"

"Well, now that you've got me thinking about it . . . When I walked my friend Giovanni, who was the last to leave, out to his car, and Giovanni turned on the headlights, I clearly saw a man at the edge of the water."

"Was he fishing?"

"I don't think so."

"What was he doing?"

"Nothing. He was just standing there. I got a pretty good look at him because Giovanni didn't leave immediately; we kept discussing the last game. He was a rather tall man, with slightly hunched shoulders . . . With one hand he was holding up a bicycle by the handlebars . . ."

"A bicycle?"

"Yes. And he had a cap on his head."

In the four days that followed, there were four more burglaries.

They couldn't figure out how the burglar was getting inside people's homes. He seemed able to pass through walls, like a ghost.

And he burgled in proportion to what his victims had to offer. If they were poor, he never took more than a thousand lire; if they were well-off, he would steal twenty or thirty thousand lire, but never more than that.

The last person to be robbed, one Signor Osvaldo Belladonna, said that he'd gone to bed after midnight, but had first opened the window to air the room out a little. Looking onto the street, he'd seen a man in a cap chaining his bicycle to a lamppost.

"What are we going to do?" asked Augello.

"What do you want to do?" Montalbano snapped at him. "Arrest every man in town who wears a cap and rides a bicycle? Post guards outside every house?"

He'd been silent and surly for days, to the point that Livia was threatening to go home to Boccadasse. Not having the slightest idea how to catch the burglar put him in a bad mood.

"No, but . . ." Augello insisted.

"But what? If you have any ideas, then take over the case!"

Fazio walked in.

"So, how's your father?" Montalbano and Augello asked almost in unison.

"In pretty good shape. They did every kind of test imaginable in Palermo, but he has to remain under observation and take a whole bunch of medications. Any new developments here?"

Montalbano didn't answer. It was up to Augello to tell him about all the burglaries. When he had finished, Fazio sat there, lost in thought.

"So?" the inspector prodded him.

"I just bet . . ." Fazio said under his breath.

"Talk louder," said Montalbano.

"Could I call my father?" Fazio asked, still lost in thought.

"Go ahead."

Fazio got up and dialed the number. He seemed excited, to the point that he forgot to turn on the speakerphone.

"Papa? Hi, it's me. Listen, do you remember the time you told me about a house burglar, a master lockpicker? . . . What was his name? Michele Gangitano? And he always got around by bicycle and was always wearing a cap on his head . . . Yeah, yeah . . . Any idea what ever became of him? Oh, he was sentenced to five years? Okay, thanks, Papa. Yes, yes, lots of love."

He set down the receiver and said:

"They must have released him. I'll go try and confirm. I'll be right back."

He went out. Montalbano and Augello sat there staring at each other and didn't say a word until Fazio returned, smiling.

"It's definitely him. Michele Gangitano. He was released twenty days ago, after serving out his sentence."

"So what are we going to do now?" said Augello, repeating the usual refrain.

Montalbano didn't have to think twice.

"Fazio, go and see where he lives and inform him that he must come in to the station at four o'clock this afternoon. And I want the both of you to be present, too."

"But you can't arrest him," said Augello.

"That's the furthest thing from my mind."

"So why have him come here?"

"Dunno."

Michele Gangitano was quite punctual, arriving at four o'clock sharp. Montalbano had him come into his office at once. Augello and Fazio were already there with him.

Gangitano was a tall, lanky man of about sixty, well-dressed, with slightly hunched shoulders and a melancholy air. He didn't have a single hair on his head, as they saw when he doffed his cap, which he now held in his hands.

He was perfectly calm and didn't even seem curious to know why he'd been called in.

"Please sit down," said Montalbano, indicating the empty chair in front of his desk.

Augello was in the other chair, while Fazio was sitting on the little sofa.

"Signor Gangitano, aren't you wondering why I called you in here?"

"I am, but it's not up to me."

"What's not up to you?"

"To be the first to speak. That's up to you, sir."

Signor Gangitano was apparently too familiar with police stations, carabinieri headquarters, and courtrooms not to respect the rules of procedure.

"I called you in here because I wanted to meet you. I've heard about you, and so I became curious."

Nobody was expecting what Gangitano said next, with a forced smile that came out looking more like a grimace.

"And I wanted to meet you, too. I heard a lot about you in prison."

"Good things or bad?"

"As with any other man."

"Meaning?"

"Some said good things, some said bad. But more said good things, including some people you'd arrested yourself."

"Speaking of which, can you tell me what you were convicted of? I haven't seen the documents. Burglary?"

Gangitano looked surprised.

"Burglary? Why do you say that? Who told you that? I was never convicted of burglary."

Montalbano felt bewildered. And without even looking at them, he already knew that Augello and Fazio were sitting there in shock.

"Never?"

"Never! You can look at my police record if you don't believe me. But I can tell you myself everything that's on it. I've got four convictions. The first was when I was a hot-blooded youth of twenty and got in trouble for brawling, a silly scuffle over a girl; the second was for embezzlement; the third for false testimony; and the fourth and last, when I was forty-five, for something that would take too long to explain."

"Tell me about it anyway."

"My brother-in-law, a father of two—"

"I'm sorry, but do you mean your wife's brother or your sister's husband?"

"My sister's husband. I've never been married. Can I continue?"

"Yes, sorry for interrupting. Go on."

"My brother-in-law, who was a stonemason, fell from a scaffold and was permanently paralyzed. But the contractor claimed that it was my brother-in-law's fault for not being careful, whereas in fact there were no safety measures taken at all at the work site. The judge, as it turns out, was having an affair with the contractor's wife and upheld his claims. So my brother-in-law was reduced to begging on the streets. Or limited to the little that I could pass on to him. So one day I waited outside the courthouse for the judge, and when he came out I bashed his face in."

"So you were reacting to an injustice?"

"That's absolutely right."

"And do you find it right, for example, for someone who has honestly earned a little money to be robbed?"

Gangitano squirmed a little in his chair, and his mood seemed to change from melancholy to distress.

"Are you, er, speaking academically?"

"Of course."

"Then my answer is: It depends."

"On what?"

"On the burglar's intentions, on his reasons for taking money that is not his."

"Explain."

"If somebody steals for the pleasure of it or to get money to throw around, then it's wrong. But if somebody steals to get the little bit he needs to eat or to help someone else in need, and not one lira more, then, I'm sure you'll understand, that changes everything."

"And you yourself will understand that, even if that changes everything for you, it changes nothing in the eyes of the law. A thief is still a thief."

"And that's the injustice of the justice system. Which, even when it grants you extenuating circumstances, still sends you to prison. All that changes is the amount of time you're inside. A judge once claimed that judges are like medical doctors: They treat the ills of society just as the doctors treat the ills of people's bodies. And I started laughing."

"Why?"

"Inspector Montalbano, there is no penal code for illnesses. Every sick person is a separate case. And the doctor treats him according to how the illness manifests in the body he's treating. And the medicine he gives to one person will be different from the medicine he gives to another who is suffering from the same illness. Whereas the law is the same for everyone."

"No, Gangitano, that's not what that statement means."

"I know what it means. But will you still tell me the law is the same for everyone if I tell you my brother-in-law's story all over again?"

The inspector figured it was best to change the subject.

"What's your judgment of the sentences you were given?"

"There's nothing for me to judge. I screwed up and I paid for it, that's all there is to it."

"So should I conclude that you harbor no desire for revenge against the criminal justice system for your jail time?"

"For my jail time, no. But, still speaking academically, if I were by chance to do anything illegal, I wouldn't be doing it out of spite or vendetta."

"I thank you for coming in. I am sure we'll meet again," said Montalbano, standing up.

"It's been very interesting for me, too. And, like you, I'm also certain we'll meet again."

"Fazio, please show Signor Gangitano out," the inspector said as he held out his hand to the visitor.

Gangitano shook it, gave a half bow to Augello, and left with Fazio.

"So what did you gain from that?" asked Mimì.

"Knowing your adversary is always a point gained. Gangitano's a shrewd, intelligent man, and not violent . . ."

"But he bashed a judge in the face!"

"Mimì, let me tell you something in confidence, man to man: I would have done the same thing. On top of that—and this is very important—he doesn't steal simply for the thrill of defying chance."

"Why is that so important?"

"Because it means he's methodical, and a creature of habit. That is, he's not a hothead who acts on impulse."

Fazio came in.

"What did you think?" he asked.

"I can say only one thing: I'll be very sorry the day I arrest him."

3

"Aside from how sorry you'll feel," said Augello, "at this point we're in a position to cure him of his bad habit. We can grab him whenever we want."

Montalbano looked at him with a mocking smile.

"Oh, yeah? How?"

"Easy. And I'm surprised you haven't thought of it yourself. Fazio, you've seen where he lives?"

"Yeah, when I went to get him to bring him here. I had to go in person, since he hasn't got a phone. He lives in a kind of old garage in Via Lampedusa, at number eighteen."

"Were you able to see whether he keeps his customary bicycle inside or outside?"

"Outside. Attached to a pole with a little chain."

"So, are you going to tell us about this plan of yours?" the inspector prodded him.

"My plan is the following: Tonight we post one of our men outside his place from midnight to five a.m. As soon as Gangitano comes out and grabs his bike, our man will follow him, without being seen, and when the guy breaks into some building to rob somebody, our guy will wait for him outside and arrest him when he comes out with the booty still fresh in his pockets."

"Okay," said Montalbano. "We'll do as you say. Even though I'm totally convinced it will only be a waste of time. Fazio, you decide which cop to send."

The following day Officer Crispino confirmed that Gangitano stayed in his garage the whole night, and Officer Misuraca said the same thing the day after that.

On the other hand, on the morning of that second day, at around nine o'clock, a certain Signora Adelaide Tripepi came into the station. She owned a fruit-and-vegetable stand with prices that would have made a high-society jeweler blanch.

She was rather upset and speaking in less than the most elegant of fashions.

"The fuckin' asshole ripped me off for five thousand lire!"

With some effort they managed to learn that the previous

evening, before going to bed, Signora Adelaide had put ten thousand lire in her purse, because she had to make a payment the following day.

"Where do you keep it?"

"Keep what? The purse? When I go to sleep I put it on a chair at the foot of the bed."

"Do you live alone?"

"No, sir, I live with my husband. But he works as a night watchman, so he's not there during the night."

"Go on."

As soon as she got to the market that morning, the signora realized there was only five thousand lire left in her purse.

"Don't you think it's possible the other five thousand could have fallen out on your way to the market?"

"But I live in Via Lampedusa, which is a long way from the market! I always take the car to go there. If the money had fallen out like you say, I would have found it in the car, don't you think?"

"Where did you say you lived, Signora?"

"Via Lampedusa, number one."

Montalbano, Augello, and Fazio all exchanged glances. This was clearly the work of Gangitano.

"Fazio, please take the lady's statement, then call Officer Misuraca and bring him back here to me."

———

"Misuraca, tell us exactly what you saw from your observation post."

"It was a good lookout point, Inspector. I could surveil the rolling garage door and the bicycle tied to the pole."

"Did you walk around the garage before taking up your position?"

"Yes. It has no rear exit."

"Not even a window?"

"There's a little window."

"With a grate over it?"

"No."

"Now think hard. Could a thin man pass through it?"

Misuraca thought about this for a moment.

"Maybe, if he practiced."

"And that's exactly what our friend Gangitano did," the inspector concluded. "And since he couldn't take his bicycle, he went and robbed a house on the same street as his, just a short walk away. Didn't I tell you, Mimì, that he's a very clever, experienced man? At any rate, we'll carry on. We'll post two guards now, even though I'm sure nothing will happen tonight."

And indeed nothing happened that night, as far as the thief was concerned.

Something big did occur, however, and pushed the case of the burglaries into the background.

That night, the twenty-year-old daughter of a wealthy entrepreneur from Montelusa with powerful political friends was kidnapped for ransom. The commissioner was under severe pressure to get the girl freed as quickly as possible, and therefore he ordered all the police commissariats in the province to devote all their efforts to the case.

And so the surveillance on Gangitano was lifted.

"But, really, what, in concrete terms, are we supposed to be doing about this kidnapping?" Augello asked Montalbano.

"What do you want me to say, Mimì? Go around and talk to the usual informants, send a few of our patrols out into the countryside, stop and question a few suspects . . ."

"And keep your eyes and ears wide open . . ." Fazio continued.

Augello shook his head.

"I don't think that's going to get us anywhere."

"Those are orders, Mimì."

Five evenings later, Montalbano went home, scarfed down the *sarde a beccafico* Adelina had made for him, then ducked into the bathroom to wash his hands.

Walking past his bedroom he noticed there was something that didn't look right. Taking a better look, he realized what it was.

The framed photo of Livia that she'd wanted him to keep on his bedside table was gone.

It must have fallen on the floor.

Going over to the nightstand, Montalbano looked carefully at the floor around it.

No photo.

It wasn't under the bed, either.

Where could it have gone?

Then he thought that perhaps it had fallen as Adelina was dusting, the glass had broken, and the housekeeper had taken it to get repaired.

Unable to resist, he decided to call her up.

Adelina swore up and down that the whole time she was in the house, the photo was on the bedside table.

After wasting another half hour searching for it in the most unlikely places, he phoned Livia.

"Did you by any chance take that picture of you back home with you?"

"Why would I do that? I put it on your bedside table."

"Well, it's no longer there."

"Have you looked under the table and bed?"

"Of course!"

"Adelina must have removed it because she hates me."

"I guess that must be it," said Montalbano, cutting things short.

He didn't feel like getting into an argument over Adelina. Also because—even though he didn't want to admit it—Livia was probably right.

The following morning, when he opened his eyes, the first thing he saw was Livia's picture on the bedside table.

And he understood everything.

When he got back home the following evening he set the table out on the veranda and ate what Adelina had prepared for him. Then he went back inside, sat down in front of the TV, and watched a spy movie in which he understood not a thing. At a quarter to midnight, he rang Livia.

"Did you find my picture?"

"Yes, it had fallen behind the nightstand."

At midnight he turned out all the lights in the house, but instead of going to bed, he went and sat out on the veranda.

He'd brought his cigarettes and lighter out with him, but since it was a dark night he decided not to smoke. The red dot of the burning cigarette end would have been visible from a distance.

He sat outside in the pitch darkness without moving, ears pricked up and ready to catch the slightest sound.

In spite of this, he still didn't hear him arrive. He didn't become aware of his presence until the man was on the veranda, one step away from him. He'd been quieter than a cat.

"Good evening."

"Good evening."

"Were you waiting for me?"

"Of course. After your little comedy with the photo . . . Have a seat."

Gangitano sat down beside him on the bench.

"Forgive me for taking the liberty of entering your house, but it would have been careless to phone you at the office, and I thought that this way you would understand that I needed to talk to you in person, with no one else around."

"Well, here I am. Now talk."

"There's no point in dragging this out with you, so I'll get straight to the point. The other evening, when I saw that you'd lifted the surveillance, I went back to work."

He called burglary "work." And, if you really thought about it, for a professional thief, burglary was indeed work.

"I wanted to break into the home of Mascolo, the lawyer. Do you know him?"

"I've heard about him. He's a two-bit lawyer of little worth. He normally defends small-time hoods, purse snatch-ers . . ."

"I think he's biting off more than he can chew."

"Why do you say that?"

"Listen to me for a minute. The lawyer is separated from his wife and lives alone. When I went into his house I heard him snoring in the bedroom. I headed for that room, but when I got to the door, I heard a telephone ring. To me it was like a machine-gun burst, believe me. I froze. The lawyer turned on the light and answered the phone, which was on his bedside table. He couldn't see me, because I was outside the room. I clearly heard everything he said. And I can repeat it to you word for word. And this is why I decided to come here to your place and tell you everything."

He paused.

"Kidnapping has always seemed to me like a most cowardly thing to do, especially kidnapping a woman or child."

Montalbano held his breath. He was afraid to interrupt Gangitano's monologue.

"First the lawyer said, 'Hello?' and then sat there in silence, listening. Then all at once he started yelling, saying that the girl must not be moved for any reason, that the place where they were hiding her was perfectly safe, and that to take her to the Faraci grotto would be insane, with all the patrols everywhere making rounds . . . Then he calmed down and said that he would write the ransom letter and send it himself within three days. And he hung up. He turned off the light, and a short while later was snoring again."

"And what did you do?"

"I left."

"Did you steal anything?"

"No, nothing."

"Why not?"

"Because I realized that if he noticed that a stranger had

been in his house, he might become suspicious that the person had overheard his phone call."

"Very well done."

"Thank you. And now, with your permission . . ."

Montalbano heard him standing up.

"Wait."

"What is it?"

"You do realize, don't you, that the information you've given me isn't enough to allow me to make a move?"

"Dear Inspector, I did what I was able to do."

"It's not enough."

"What else do you want from me?"

"To go back into Mascolo's house."

4

Gangitano was taken aback. Then he said:

"Well, if that's an order . . ."

"When did you go into Mascolo's house?"

"Night before last."

"When exactly did he tell his playmates that he would write and send the ransom letter?"

"Three days later."

"So there's still time."

"To do what?"

"Maybe the letter's still there, in the house. It's the only evidence we have at this point. But you'll have to go back there again tonight."

"But—"

"No buts," said Montalbano, not letting him finish. By now he'd made up his mind and there was no way he would change it. "Have you got all your tools with you?"

"Yessir."

"And for once you should go without your bicycle."

"It's too far to go on foot."

"Want to take my car?"

"But I don't know how to drive!"

"I'll take you myself."

Gangitano felt like he'd entered a madhouse.

"What? You'll take me to commit a burglary?"

"There won't be any burgling."

"So what are we going there to do?"

"You only have to see if you can find the letter or some other thing that will connect the lawyer to the kidnapping. If you do see it, then leave it right where it is and come and tell me."

"Come to the police station?"

"What police station?! I'll be waiting for you in my car, outside the lawyer's front door."

"So, you'll be my lookout, sort of?"

"Exactly. Now let's not waste any more time."

Before going out, the inspector put a piece of paper in his pocket with the phone numbers of the coordinator of the investigation into the kidnapping, Vice Commissioner Martorana.

━━━━━

Antonio Mascolo, attorney-at-law, lived on the second floor of a five-story building not far from the center of town, at number 5 on a short but wide street that was called, for reasons unknown, Via Stromboli. It was a street of shops and stores and therefore all they saw were metal shutters. There was nobody about. The inspector looked at his watch. It was a few minutes before two.

Gangitano dug a small metal ring out of his jacket pocket with some ten or so strangely shaped keys attached to it.

"That's all you've got?" asked Montalbano, slightly disappointed.

"Yes. But if you know how to use them, they work miracles."

Then he looked at the inspector and said:

"I'm going in."

"I'll wait for you outside."

"I hope you're not just going to arrest me when you see me running out."

"No need to worry about that."

Gangitano got out and walked up to the front door. Montalbano didn't have time to count to ten before the guy was already inside with the door closed behind him.

And at that moment the inspector, who until then had felt calm and untroubled, suddenly began to feel extremely nervous.

By ten after two he'd already looked at his watch a good twenty times.

By two-twenty he'd smoked seven cigarettes.

By two-thirty he began to feel itchy all over his body, as if he'd been bitten by a thousand ants.

By two-forty he was biting his nails thinking that the lawyer had woken up, caught Gangitano, and . . .

He had to save him.

He didn't think twice. Opening the glove compartment,

he grabbed his revolver, got out of the car, and dashed to the front door. He was going to press every buzzer until someone answered.

At that very moment the door came open, and Gangitano appeared before the inspector.

"What the hell are you doing, Inspector? Get back in the car!"

Mortified, Montalbano obeyed, sticking his gun in his jacket pocket. Gangitano sat down beside him.

"I wasn't able to find anything at all—that's what took me so long. But then, when I was about to give up, I found it."

"Found what?"

"The letter."

Montalbano had to restrain himself from hugging the man.

"Where was it?"

"In the pocket of an overcoat hanging in the vestibule. It was already in its envelope, which isn't sealed, however. Since I had a flashlight with me and was wearing gloves, I took it out and started reading the first few words. He definitely wanted to send it this morning."

"All right. Now come with me."

"Where to?"

"To the lawyer's bedroom—at which point you'll slip away."

Montalbano was amazed at the skill with which Gangitano manipulated his strange keys. He was a real master. Ten minutes later they were in the vestibule of the lawyer's apartment. They could hear him snoring, even from that distance. Montalbano, who wasn't wearing gloves, signaled to Gangitano to take the letter out of the coat pocket and open it so he could read it. Gangitano grabbed the envelope, pulled out the letter, and held it in front of the inspector's eyes, lighting it up with his flashlight. The first line, written in block capitals, was quite enough:

IF YOU WANT TO SEE YOUR DAUGHTER ALIVE AGAIN . . .

He had Gangitano put it back in the envelope and then whispered to him:

"Now get out of here."

Without a word, the man opened the door, went out, and closed it again without a sound. Montalbano found himself in utter darkness. He advanced slowly, guided by the lawyer's snoring.

When he got to the bedroom, he took out his gun, feeling the wall with the other hand until he found the light switch, which he flicked on.

Mascolo the lawyer kept right on snoring. The inspector sat down in a chair at the foot of the bed, then took his pistol and knocked the butt against a spot on the blanket that corresponded with the lawyer's knee.

Mascolo finally woke up, eyelids fluttering, sat up in bed and, seeing the barrel of a handgun pointed at him, put his hands up in terror.

"Who—who are you?"

"That doesn't matter. What matters is that you keep perfectly quiet, or I'll shoot you," Montalbano said coolly.

"For heaven's sake, don't do anything to me," said the lawyer. "I've got three million in the—"

"I'm not interested in your money."

Mascolo became even more terrified.

"Then what do you want?"

Montalbano didn't answer. He just stood up, took from his pocket the piece of paper with Vice Commissioner Martorana's number on it, and dialed it from the phone on the man's nightstand.

"Martorana? Montalbano here. Sorry to bother you at this hour of the night, but I'm calling about the girl who was kidnapped. I think I've located one of the gang. I suggest you go within the next fifteen minutes to Via Stromboli, number five, in Vigàta. The name on the buzzer outside is Mascolo, attorney-at-law. Come by yourself, no sirens or squad cars, and you may just manage to catch them all by surprise. I'll wait for you here. Hurry."

It all went as the inspector had foreseen. The girl was freed the following day and the whole gang was arrested. At the press conference Vice Commissioner Martorana said a good deal of the credit must go to his colleague Montalbano. But he didn't say why.

The commissioner, on the other hand, wanted to know.

"Really, Montalbano, you're not going to tell me the knowledge that the letter was in the pocket of the unsuspected lawyer Mascolo's overcoat came to you in a revelation from the Holy Spirit!"

"No, not the Holy Spirit, but—"

"Listen, at the very least we need to get our story straight to tell to the judge!"

"Mr. Commissioner, it was a burglar who broke into the lawyer's house who—"

"Come on, Montalbano! Don't give me such rot! Do you think I'm stupid or something? Find a better story."

All at once Montalbano realized that no one would ever believe what had really happened.

"Okay, it was an informant of mine. But I don't want to burn him. He's too valuable."

"Good God! Did you have to go that far? We'll only tell his name to the judge, and we'll arrange it so he won't even be questioned. What's his name?"

"Agostino Lobue," the inspector said, poker-faced.

But the game with Gangitano wasn't over yet, and the inspector wanted to end it. He got his chance when, five days after the girl was freed, her father, the engineer Di Bartolo, went to the station to thank him. Montalbano found the man quite likable.

"Clearly, if not for your informant and your immediate intervention . . ."

Montalbano at this moment had an inspiration.

"Do you really want to know how it happened? It actually wasn't an informant who told me, but . . ."

And he told him everything.

Signor Di Bartolo remained silent for a moment, then said:

"Listen, tell Signor Gangitano that if he wants to earn an honest living, all he has to do is come to my office."

That very same evening, at eleven o'clock, Montalbano left his house, got in his car, and headed for Via Lampedusa, pulling up a short distance away from Gangitano's garage. Shortly after midnight, the rolling door was opened. Gangitano came out, reclosed the door, got on his bicycle, and pedaled quickly away. Montalbano followed him in his car. When he got to a street not far from police headquarters, Gangitano stopped, got off his bike, leaned it against a tree, headed for the front door of a three-story building, opened it, went inside, and closed the door behind him. Montalbano sat tight in his car, then at a certain point got out, fired up a cigarette, and headed for the same door. He hadn't had time to finish smoking it when the door opened, and out came Gangitano, who, upon seeing the inspector, stopped dead in his tracks.

"Goo—good evening," he managed to say.

"If you say so . . ." said Montalbano. "How much did you steal this time?"

"Two thousand lire."

"Put the money back where you found it. I'll be waiting for you here."

"What for?"

"To arrest you and take you to the station."

"Okay," said Gangitano.

He returned five minutes later.

"Get in the car."

Gangitano obeyed. When they arrived outside the station house, Montalbano stopped the car.

"And you know what? In the report I'm going to write that you resisted arrest and struck me with your fist."

Gangitano looked at him in shock.

"I certainly wasn't expecting that, not from you. Why do you want to send me to jail?"

"I don't want to send you to jail. I want to present you with a choice. Either I arrest you now and you spend a few more years in jail, or tomorrow you call up, on my behalf, Engineer Di Bartolo, who's the father of the kidnapped girl."

"And what's Di Bartolo going to do?"

"He's going to give you an honest job."

Gangitano sat there for a long time, staring at Montalbano. Then he took the ring with the keys out of his pocket and set it down in the inspector's lap.

"You can keep these as a souvenir. Tomorrow morning I'll do as you say and give him a call. Good night."

"Good night," replied Montalbano, opening the door to let him out.

Notes

8 "A pittance. About twenty million lire": As this story is supposed to be taking place in the early 1980s, twenty million lire at the time was worth a little under twenty thousand dollars.

70 As he was heading for Vigàta he wondered what mysterious reason Cosentino could have had for naming his fishing boat after a Spanish king: To Sicilians, long under Spanish dominion, the name Carlo III might naturally call to mind Carlos Tercero (1716–1788), king of Spain, and ruler of Sicily and Naples as well.

93 And he found Toto Cutugno singing "*Con la chitarra in mano*," from "L'Italiano," which he'd presented at the San Remo festival the year before: In 1983, that is. Thus the present story is supposed to be taking place in 1984, when Montalbano is thirty-four years old. Cutugno's song is generally known by its title "L'Italiano."

193 "You been talking to crows or something?": "To talk to crows" (*parlare con le ciavole*) is a Sicilian expression indicating being privy to information as if by supernatural means.

247 ". . . only a thousand lire?": That is, a little under a dollar at the time.

Notes by Stephen Sartarelli

MONTALBANO'S FIRST CASE AND OTHER STORIES

Andrea Camilleri has selected twenty-one short stories that follow Italy's famous detective through the highlight cases of his career. This collection is an essential addition to any Inspector Montalbano fan's bookshelf and a wonderful introduction to the internationally bestselling series.

HUNTING SEASON

In 1880s Vigàta, a stranger comes to town to open a pharmacy, looking to make his fortune. Fofò turns out to be the son of a man legendary for having a magic garden stocked with plants that could cure any ailment—a man who was found murdered years ago. A brilliant, bawdy comedy that will surprise even the most die-hard Montalbano fans.

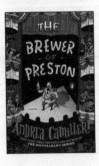

THE BREWER OF PRESTON

1870s Sicily. Much to the displeasure of Vigàta's stubborn populace, the town has just been unified under the Kingdom of Italy. Eugenio Bortuzzi has been named the regional representative from the Italian government, but the unruly Sicilians don't care much for the mediocre opera he's hell-bent on producing, and the Vigàtese are revving up to wreak havoc on the performance's opening night.

Ⓟ PENGUIN BOOKS

ANDREA CAMILLERI

"Camilleri is as crafty and charming a writer
as his protagonist is an investigator."
—*The Washington Post Book World*

For a complete list of titles,
please visit www.prh.com/andreacamilleri

PENGUIN BOOKS